Dakota Cassidy | Witch Slapped

Witchless in Seattle Mysteries, Book 1

Witch Slapped

TODAY BESTSELLING AUTHOR

DAKOTA CASSIDY

Published 2017 by Dakota Cassidy.

ISBN: ISBN-13: 978-1545192078

Copyright © 2017, Dakota Cassidy.

All rights reserved.

No part of this publication may be reproduced, stored in a retrieval system, or transmitted in any form or by any means, electronic, mechanical, recording, or otherwise, without the prior written permission of Dakota Cassidy.

This book is a work of fiction. Any similarity to actual persons, living or dead, locales, or events is wholly coincidental. The names, characters, dialogue, and events in this book are from the author's imagination and should not to be construed as real.

Manufactured in the USA.

Email dakota@dakotacassidy.com with questions or inquiries.

Witchless in Seattle

Witch Slapped

If you're joining me for the first time, welcome to Ebenezer Falls, Washington, a fictional suburb of Seattle, where my heroine, Stevie Cartwright, has gone to lick her witchless wounds! This cozy mystery and the ensuing series to come is a spinoff of my Paris, Texas, romance series. If you've not visited the whacky happenings in Paris, fear not, darling readers! This series is completely stand-alone. If you've read Paris, expect to see some familiar faces dropping in from time to time.

I also hope you'll join me for *Quit Your Witchin'*, Book 2, and *Dewitched*, Book 3 in this series, releasing each month for the next two months.

No matter how you got here, thanks so much for joining Stevie and company on their journey to solve afterlife mysteries and her search to regain her witchy powers!

Also, enormous thanks to Mikell Mcdermott who, out of the blue, threw this awesome title up on my Facebook page—you rock! My BFF forever and ever, Renee George, for her endless advice, and my buddy Michelle Hoppe for her guidance.

And to Arwen Lynch Poe, for her amazing tarot card help and a reading for my character, which I'm still blown away by! I hope you'll check her out on YouTube http://www.youtube.com/arwen61

Dakota XXOO

Dakota Cassidy | Witch Slapped

Acknowledgements

Cover: Valerie Tibbs, Tibbs Design

Editor: Kelli Collins

Chapter 1

"Left, Stevie! Left!" my familiar, Belfry, bellowed, flapping his teeny bat wings in a rhythmic whir against the lash of wind and rain. "No, your other left! If you don't get this right sometime soon, we're gonna end up resurrecting the entire population of hell!"

I repositioned him in the air, moving my hand to the left, my fingers and arms aching as the icy rains of Seattle in February battered my face and my last clean outfit. "Are you sure it was *here* that the voice led you? Like right in this spot? Why would a ghost choose a cliff on a hill in the middle of Ebenezer Falls as a place to strike up a conversation?"

"Stevie Cartwright, in your former witch life, did the ghosts you once spent more time with than the living always choose convenient locales to do their talking? As I recall, that loose screw Ferdinand Santos decided to make an appearance at the gynecologist. Remember? It was all stirrups and forceps and gabbing about you going to his wife to tell her where he hid the toenail clippers. That's only one example. Shall I list more?"

Sometimes, in my former life as a witch, those who'd gone to the Great Beyond contacted me to help them settle up a score, or reveal information they took to the grave but felt guilty about taking. Some scores and guilty consciences were worthier than others.

"Fine. Let's forget about convenience and settle for getting the job done because it's forty degrees and dropping, you're going to catch your death, and I can't spend all day on a rainy cliff just because you're sure someone is trying to contact me using *you* as my conduit. You aren't like rabbit ears on a TV, buddy. And let's not forget the fact that we're unemployed, if you'll recall. We need a job, Belfry. We need big, big job before my savings turns to ashes and joins the pile that was once known as my life."

"Higher!" he demanded. Then he asked, "Speaking of ashes, on a scale of one to ten, how much do you hate Baba Yaga today? You know, now that we're a month into this witchless gig?"

Losing my witch powers was a sore subject I tried in quiet desperation to keep on the inside.

I puffed an icy breath from my lips, creating a spray from the rain splashing into my mouth. "I don't hate Baba," I replied easily.

Almost too easily.

The answer had become second nature. I responded the same way every time anyone asked when referring to the witch community's fearless, ageless leader, Baba Yaga, who'd shunned me right out of my former life in Paris, Texas, and back to my roots in a suburb of Seattle.

I won't lie. That had been the single most painful moment of my life. I didn't think anything could top being left at the altar by Warren the Wayward Warlock. Forget losing a fiancé. I had the witch literally slapped right out of me. I lost my entire being. Everything I've ever known.

Belfry made his wings flap harder and tipped his head to the right, pushing his tiny skull into the wind. "But you no likey. Baba booted you out of Paris, Stevie. Shunned you like you'd never even existed."

Paris was the place to be for a witch if living out loud was your thing. There was no hiding your magic, no fear of a human uprising or being burned at the stake out of paranoia. Everyone in the small town of Paris was paranormal, though primarily it was made up of my own kind.

Some witches are just as happy living where humans are the majority of the population. They don't mind keeping their powers a secret, but I came to love carrying around my wand in my back pocket just as naturally as I'd carry my lipstick in my purse.

I really loved the freedom to practice white magic anywhere I wanted within the confines of Paris and its rules, even if I didn't love feeling like I lived two feet from the fiery jaws of Satan.

But Belfry had taken my ousting from the witch community much harder than me—or maybe I should say he's more vocal about it than me.

So I had to ask. "Do you keep bringing up my universal shunning to poke at me, because you get a kick out of seeing my eyes at their puffiest after a good, hard cry? Or do you ask to test the waters because there's some witch event Baba's hosting that you want to go to with all your little familiar friends and you know the subject is a sore one for me this early in the 'Stevie isn't a witch anymore' game?"

Belfry's small body trembled. "You hurt my soul, Cruel One. I would never tease about something so delicate. It's neither. As your familiar, it's my job to know where your emotions rank. I can't read you like I used to because—"

"Because I'm not on the same wavelength as you. Our connection is weak and my witchy aura is fading. Yadda, yadda, yadda. I get it. Listen, Bel, I don't hate BY. She's a good leader. On the other hand, I'm not inviting her over for girls' night and braiding her hair either. She did what she had to in accordance with the white witch way. I also get that. She's the head witch in charge and it's her duty to protect the community."

"Protect-schmotect. She was over you like a champion hurdler. In a half second flat."

Belfry was bitter-schmitter.

"Things have been dicey in Paris as of late, with a lot of change going on. You know that as well as I do. I just happened to be unlucky enough to be the proverbial straw to break Baba's camel back. She made me the example to show everyone how she protects us…er, *them*. So could we not talk about her or my defunct powers or my old life anymore? Because if we don't look to the future and get me employed, we're going to have to make curtains out of your tiny wings to cover the window of our box under the bridge."

"Wait! There he is! Hold steady, Stevie!" he yelled into the wind.

We were out on this cliff in the town I'd grown up in because Belfry claimed someone from the afterlife—someone British—was trying to contact me, and as he followed the voice, it was clearest here. In the freezing rain…

Also in my former life, from time to time, I'd helped those who'd passed on solve a mystery. Now that I was unavailable for comment, they tried reaching me via Belfry.

The connection was always hazy and muddled, it came and went, broken and spotty, but Belfry wasn't ready to let go of our former life. So more often than not, over the last month since I'd been booted from the community, as the afterlife grew anxious about my vacancy, the dearly departed sought any means to connect with me.

Belfry was the most recent "any means."

"Madam *Who*?" Belfry squeaked in his munchkin voice, startling me. "Listen up, matey, when you contact a medium, you gotta turn up the volume!"

"Belfryyy!" I yelled when a strong wind picked up, lashing at my face and making my eyes tear. "This is moving toward ridiculous. Just tell whoever it is that I can't come to the phone right now due to poverty!"

He shrugged me off with an impatient flap of his wings. "Wait! Just one more sec—what's that? *Zoltar?* What in all the bloomin' afterlife is a Zoltar?" Belfry paused and, I'd bet, held his breath while he waited for an answer—and then he let out a long, exasperated squeal of frustration before his tiny body went limp.

Which panicked me. Belfry was prone to drama-ish tendencies at the best of times, but the effort he was putting into being my conduit of sorts had been taking a toll. He was all I had, my last connection to anything supernatural. I couldn't bear losing him.

So I yanked him to my chest and tucked him into my soaking-wet sweater as I made a break for the hotel we were a week from being evicted right out of.

"Belfry!" I clung to his tiny body, rubbing my thumbs over the backs of his wings.

Belfry is a cotton ball bat. He's two inches from wing to wing of pure white bigmouth and minute yellow ears and snout, with origins stemming from Honduras, Nicaragua, and Costa Rica, where it's warm and humid.

Since we'd moved here to Seattle from the blazing-hot sun of Paris, Texas, he'd struggled with the cooler weather.

I was always finding ways to keep him warm, and now that he'd taxed himself by staying too long in the crappy weather we were having, plus using all his familiar energy to figure out who was trying to contact me, his wee self had gone into overload.

I reached for the credit card key to our hotel room in my skirt pocket and swiped it, my hands shaking. Slamming the door shut with the heel of my foot, I ran to the bathroom, flipped on the lights and set Belfry on a fresh white towel. His tiny body curled inward, leaving his wings tucked under him as pinhead-sized drops of water dripped on the towel.

Grabbing the blow dryer on the wall, I turned the setting to low and began swishing it over him from a safe distance so as not to knock him off the vanity top. "Belfry! Don't you poop on me now, buddy. I need you!" Using my index and my thumb, I rubbed along his rounded back, willing warmth into him.

"To the right," he ordered.

My fingers stiffened as my eyes narrowed, but I kept rubbing just in case.

He groaned. "Ahh, yeah. Riiight there."

"Belfry?"

"Yes, Wicked One?"

"Not the time to test my devotion."

"Are you fragile?"

"I wouldn't use the word fragile. But I would use mildly agitated and maybe even raw. If you're just joking around, knock it off. I've had all I can take in the way of shocks and upset this month."

He used his wings to push upward to stare at me with his melty chocolate eyes. "I wasn't testing your devotion. I was just depleted. Whoever this guy is, trying to get you on the line, he's determined. How did you manage to keep your fresh, dewy appearance with all that squawking in your ears all the time?"

I shrugged my shoulders and avoided my reflection in the mirror over the vanity. I didn't look so fresh and dewy anymore, and I knew it. I looked tired and devoid of interest in most everything around me. The bags under my eyes announced it to the world.

"We need to find a job, Belfry. We have exactly a week before my savings account is on E."

"So no lavish spending. Does that mean I'm stuck with the very average Granny Smith for dinner versus, say, a yummy pomegranate?"

I chuckled because I couldn't help it. I knew my laughter egged him on, but he was the reason I still got up every morning. Not that I'd ever tell him as much.

I reached for another towel and dried my hair, hoping it wouldn't frizz. "You get whatever is on the discount rack, buddy. Which should be incentive enough for you to help me find a job, lest you forgot how ripe those discounted bananas from the whole foods store really were."

"Bleh. Okay. Job. Onward ho. Got any leads?"

"The pharmacy in the center of town is looking for a cashier. It won't get us a cute house at the end of a cul-de-sac, but it'll pay for a decent enough studio. Do you want to come with or stay here and rest your weary wings?"

"Where you go, I go. I'm the tuna to your mayo."

"You have to stay in my purse, Belfry," I warned, scooping him up with two fingers to bring him to the closet with me to help me choose an outfit. "You can't wander out like you did at the farmers' market. I thought that jelly vendor was going to faint. This isn't Paris anymore. No one knows I'm a witch—" I sighed. "*Was* a witch, and no one especially knows you're a talking bat. Seattle is eclectic and all about the freedom to be you, but they haven't graduated to letting ex-witches leash their chatty bats outside of restaurants just yet."

"I got carried away. I heard 'mango chutney' and lost my teensy mind. I promise to stay in the dark hovel you call a purse—even if the British guy contacts me again."

"Forget the British guy and help me decide. Red Anne Klein skirt and matching jacket, or the less formal Blue Fly jeans and Gucci silk shirt in teal."

"You're not interviewing with Karl Lagerfeld. You're interviewing to sling sundries. Gum, potato chips, *People* magazine, maybe the occasional script for Viagra."

"It's an organic pharmacy right in that kitschy little knoll in town where all the food trucks and tattoo shops are. I'm not sure they make all-natural Viagra, but you sure sound disappointed we might have a roof over our heads."

"I'm disappointed you probably won't be wearing all those cute vintage clothes you're always buying at the thrift store if you work in a pharmacy."

"I haven't gotten the job yet, and if I do, I guess I'll just be the cutest cashier ever."

I decided on the Ann Klein. It never hurt to bring a touch of understated class, especially when the class had only cost me a total of twelve dollars.

As I laid out my wet clothes to dry on the tub and went about the business of putting on my best interview facade, I tried not to think about Belfry's broken communication with the British guy. There were times as a witch when I'd toiled over the souls who needed closure, sometimes to my detriment.

But I couldn't waste energy fretting over what I couldn't fix. And if British Guy was hoping I could help him now, he was sorely misinformed.

Maybe the next time Belfry had an otherworldly connection, I'd ask him to put everyone in the afterlife on notice that Stevie Louise Cartwright was out of order.

Grabbing my purse from the hook on the back of the bathroom door, I smoothed my hands over my skirt and squared my shoulders.

"You ready, Belfry?"

"As I'll ever be."

"Ready, set, job!"

As I grabbed my raincoat and tucked Belfry into my purse, I sent up a silent prayer to the universe that my unemployed days were numbered.

Chapter 2

I sagged against the brick façade of the pharmacy and blew out a breath of defeat as I watched the pouring rain splash into a puddle-filled pothole in the middle of the road. "Okay, so that didn't go quite as I'd hoped."

Belfry scoffed from the inside of my box-shaped purse. "It didn't go at all."

"Jeez Louise. She was like a drill sergeant." I referred to the manager of the pharmacy, who, in all her yellow-smocked militancy, had shot my application and me down like a skeet shooter.

"Uh-huh. I can't remember the last time I saw such a sourpuss. She'll need to set up camp in the laxative aisle if she keeps that up."

"I feel a little like the fates are conspiring against me, Belfry. This is the ninth job I've been turned down for. I didn't think the humiliation could be topped after yesterday's rejection. I mean, if you can't get a job at Weezie's Weenie Hut, what's left?"

"That's not the fates, Stevie. It's your resume. You *have* no resume. Humans in the real world have resumes. It looks bad that you're thirty-two and have no job history. We need to create a human you. A reinvention of sorts."

Now that really burned my britches. I did so have a job history, and I said as much when I managed to offend the manager of the pharmacy with my outraged disbelief.

Jeez. This was miserable. "I *do* have a job history, Belfry. I have ten years as a 9-1-1 dispatcher. Shouldn't that count for something?"

"Well, it might if, in the human world, people were looking for an emergency operator whose specialty was talking psychopathic warlocks off the ledge of a spell."

Yeah. Good times. I managed a snicker. "I was really good at that." Then I frowned, annoyed by the memory. My job was the very reason I was in this stinkpot of toxic waste.

"You know what I say to this, Stevie? I say bollocks!"

Somebody'd clearly been influenced by the UK this morning. "Does the British guy say that, too?"

"No. Or I don't know. I mean, he didn't when we had that hacked-up communication out there on the cliff. I just imagine that's the word he'd use for this mess we're in. If it weren't for your old job, you'd still be a witch. So again, I say bollocks and bull teats!"

"Bulls don't have teats. They're male."

"Whatever. Why won't you just listen to me and help me figure out a way to get your powers back? To prove you did nothing wrong? Then you wouldn't have to worry about getting a crummy minimum-wage job. We could do it. You and me. Just like Rizzoli and Isles. We'll find a way."

Ah my Belfry, always my little champion. "Because who knows how long that could take, and in the meantime we have nowhere to live. Besides, what's there to figure out? A council member stole my powers. Does it get any more definitive than that?"

Why was I allowing myself to be sucked into this conversation? No one wanted to relive the horror of that night less than me.

Belfry growled from inside my purse, rustling the napkin I'd tucked him into to keep him warm. "If I ever get my hands on that dirty bird council mothereffer, I'm gonna rip a hole in him!"

"With your big scary teeth?"

"Oh, shush. I can be scary."

"No doubt. So scary the word 'terrifying' should be a hyphen on your name."

"You're avoiding."

I nodded. You bet your bippy I was avoiding. "Yep."

"So now that you've been usurped by a pimply sixteen-year-old who probably still plays with his X-Men dolls—for a job even someone like *me*, with no opposable thumbs, could perform—what are you gonna do?"

"Steal his X-Men dolls and burn them in effigy?"

Belfry did his impression of maniacal laughter. "Ooo, I like this plan, Dr. Evil. Tell me more."

I was still in job-history shock. When a teenaged high school student has more work history than you do at thirty-two, a reevaluation's in order. It wasn't like I could tell the manager of the pharmacy I had more people skills than the cruise director on the *Love Boat* as a 9-1-1 operator for the paranormal.

I'd stopped my fair share of spells gone awry, earthquakes, one tsunami, two almost-shifts in the equator, countless wand lashings, a broom landing on the moon, not to mention hundreds of witch vs. warlock domestic disputes—just to name a few. Believe me, when a wand and a binding spell are involved, it's a hundred times worse than your average human 9-1-1 call.

But none of that counts anymore and if I let the pot with all my emotions about my current situation sit on the burner too long, it was sure to boil over. So I'd taken to compartmentalizing my anger and only letting it out when I couldn't feed off the energy of Belfry's rage.

He only encourages me to ball my fist and raise it to the sky in anguish. For now, that isn't helping us. Once I manage to figure out this new half of my life, I fully intend to let 'er rip.

Until then…

Pushing off the side of the building, I huffed a determined breath. "I say we go grab some lunch off the dollar menu at that food cart with the guy who makes tacos out of recycled something or other and rethink our plan of attack."

I began to walk along the cracked sidewalk, staying dry by ducking under the awnings of the various locally owned businesses that had cropped up since I'd been gone.

I wouldn't admit it to Belfry, but I'd missed the scent of the Puget Sound, the tang of water in the air, the colorful sails of the boats in the harbor, and the mountains peeking at me when the skies were clear. I loved Seattle. I never would have left to begin with if not for the job offer in Paris.

The squawk of seagulls darting through the parking lot across the street was like music to my ears. A parking lot for a fresh-fish market that hadn't been there when I'd left Seattle. Still, Ebenezer Falls was as charming and quaint as ever.

Multicolored awnings decked out each storefront, and though it was February now, the spring would bring with it spots of dappled sun and tulips by the dozen, anchoring each store's door in bright clay pots the size of barrels.

Bicyclers would stream through town in an array of festive Lycra, the streetlamp posts would sport hanging pots brimming with purple petunias and daisies, and the curbs would be lined with wrought iron tables for diners who were willing to brave the chance of rain with their alfredo.

Despite my circumstances, it was good to inhale cool, tangy air again.

As I made my way down Main Street, blinking lights from a flashing pink and green neon sign caught the corner of my eye, making me slow my roll and look upward at the twinkling bulbs, racing around the perimeter of the sign.

I stopped dead in my tracks, my galoshes splashing into a small puddle as I looked again.

Shut the front door.

Belfry rustled around in my purse, pulling himself up until his little yellow ears poked out of the rim. "What's the holdup, Boss? I'm starving," Bel asked, until he, too, read the sign on the store.

Our reflections in the big picture window mirrored one another's for a moment and then he went silent along with me.

Before he exploded. "I told you the British guy was on the up and up! Told you, told you, tolllld you!"

I reread the flashing sign. Madam Zoltar's Psychic Readings. Medium To The Heavens. Séances—Palm Readings—Tarot Cards.

Okay, so when British guy relayed the name Zoltar to Belfry, maybe he *had* heard him correctly. Then again, maybe it was just a bizarre coincidence.

Still, there was an odd tingle in my belly, like the days of old when I still had an emotion to offer other than despair and defeat.

But I wasn't so convinced yet. "Bel, c'mon. Listen, it's not that I don't believe you heard a guy ringing you up from the afterlife. You're a familiar to a defunct witch. You still have your powers. It makes sense that you'd be some sort of weird channel to my old life and maybe even some residual ghostly chatter, but what does a British guy have to do with a psychic? Especially a psychic who named herself after the one in the movie *Big*? All human psychics are full of Twinkies. You know it, I know it."

"No way are you not going in there, Stevie! No bleepin' way. I know what British Dude said, and the name Zoltar was crystal clear. Not a chance in seven hells I'm not investigating this. If you won't take me inside, I will climb right out of this musty old purse of yours and find a way in myself. Plus, I'll strike up conversations with every single person who passes by. Once they're over the shock of a talking bat, we'll talk about the weather, the price of pork bellies, we'll swap recipes and Facebook pages—"

"Okay fine!" I shouted, and then gave a surreptitious look around to be sure no one heard me yelling at my purse. "You settle down in there, Saucy Pants. Nowhere in this friendship of ours are you in charge. Got it? I'm only going in because you seem so certain this ghost is trying to tell you something rather than just testing out his afterlife voice."

"Then after you," he said with a grandiose tone.

I grabbed the handle of the glass door, hoping against hope I wasn't making the biggest mistake I'd made yet.

The smell of incense wafted to my nose immediately, almost overwhelmingly, with the scents of vanilla and a hint of sage. The odor was swiftly followed by a dozen or so obnoxious chimes attached to the door, ringing out our entry.

Belfry squeaked a cough. "Egads, is she trying to hide the scent of a corpse?"

I lifted my purse and stuck my face in my familiar's. "You pipe down," I whisper-yelled from a tight jaw. "We cannot afford another problem. Now, we're here, and I'm playing along, but I won't play so nice if we end up in the psych ward for an evaluation because I'm talking to my purse."

With a quick glance, I assessed the interior of the small store, littered with all sorts of freestanding metal shelves holding various-colored candles, each representing a meaning when you lit them.

And statues of Mary. Lots and lots of statues of Mary. One rack held healing crystals, most of which were bunk and wouldn't heal a blackhead, but I reminded myself not to judge. Everyone had to make a living, and maybe this Madam Zoltar would be the first human I'd ever encountered who really could talk to the dead.

Who was I to say, being a former witch who really *could* make a caldron bubble? I had no right to talk.

I wandered past a spinny rack with postcards, and tarot cards, too, a wall of wind chimes and dream catchers, and a back room with a gauzy purple piece of fabric separating it from the rest of the store. The store itself was lit almost solely with LED candles that ran on batteries and one dim light bulb beneath a red lampshade with beads hanging like fringe around the edges.

As I looked around, Madam Zoltar's appeared devoid of human life.

But another scent, one that rose above the incense, drifted to my nose. I knew I recognized it. I just couldn't place it. Woodsy and expensive, the cologne or perfume—I couldn't decide—lingered for a moment and then it was gone.

"Madam Zoltar?" I called out, hoping against hope she wasn't home so I could end this wild goose chase of Belfry's feeling confident I'd at least tried to humor him. I noted the employee bathroom and rapped on the door with my knuckles. "Madam Zoltar, are you in there?"

Nothing but silence greeted my ears.

I tapped the side of my purse with my nail. "See? Nobody's home. Now can we go get lunch?"

"Not on your life, sister. Put me on the counter by the cash register and let me fly, baby."

I set my purse on the glass covering the counter and shook my head. "You're absolutely not getting out of my purse. So whatever you have to do, do it from in there."

"Shh! I think I'm getting something."

I fought a roll of my eyes and waited, crossing my arms over my chest.

Belfry gasped, a tiny rasp of air, but a gasp of surprise nonetheless. "I can hear him! Pick me up and face me north, Stevie. Do it now!"

"Belfry—"

"Now!"

His tone was so urgent, I decided there was no reason to upset him if there was no one to witness his shenanigans. I scooped him into my palm and held him facing north when he suddenly stiffened.

"Do you hear him?"

Was that some kind of joke? "No, I don't hear him. I can't hear anyone from that plane anymore and you know it, Bel. Stop being cruel."

"Sorrysorrysorry. It was just instinct to ask. Forget that. He's here, Stevie. He's here!"

"Yay." I wanted to be excited for Belfry, because his excitement was infectious. Yet, I couldn't help but instead feel a pang of jealousy, and I didn't like admitting it.

Belfry burst out in a fit of giggles, making me feel incredibly left out.

"Hey, I wanna hear the joke, too."

"Oh, so now you wanna play, Mopey Gus?"

I shook my head, knocking off my raincoat hood. "No. I don't want to play. I want to eat lunch. Finish up with British Guy and let's get out of here before Madame Zoltar comes back from her lunch break and we get caught."

"I was laughing at his name."

My ears perked. "Which is?"

"Winterbottom." And then Belfry laughed again, his munchkin-like chuckle spurring my own laughter.

A giggle escaped my lips. "Winterbottom? Was he a butler?"

"Mate? Give me one second. My mean friend is making fun of your name."

I seesawed my hand, giving him a little shake. "Traitor," I muttered under my breath.

"Shhhhhh! I'm trying to hear what the fudge he's saying and he keeps fading in and out."

I let my eyes fall to the floor, a cold slab of concrete painted gray. "Sorry."

"Argh! Hold your palm up, Stevie, and your right leg. The signal's weakening."

"I will not."

"Do it!"

I reluctantly held up my right leg, noting my galoshes had seen better days.

"Say that again?" Belfry requested, his tiny body rigid with the effort to hear British Guy. "Oh boy."

Belfry's tone sounded ominous. "What's happening?"

"Just one more sec…" he trailed off as he strained forward, his wings at full mast.

My right leg began to wobble and cramp. "Can't hold on much longer, Belfry!" I gritted out.

"Just a little longer, Stevie!"

The moment Belfry begged for reprieve was the moment I tipped backward, the burning in my calf finally getting the better of me. As I toppled, I tried to hold my hand up to keep Belfry from harm.

Which was when I completely lost it and crashed into the spinny rack, knocking it over and falling against the sharply pronged wire postcard holders. "Ow!"

Postcards exploded in every direction as I rolled away from the prongs poking into my skin, but in the process somehow managed to catch the unstable metal shelf full of candles.

There was a small rumble like distant thunder before everything just collapsed in a screech of metal. One candle after the other dropped in a domino effect, some knocking me in the head, others splitting into chunky fragments.

I howled a word I can't use in polite company as the candle meant to bring your true love back to you whacked me on the noggin. Stumbling blindly from the sharp sting, I attempted to scramble upward, only to stand on a cylinder-shaped candle and, like some demented log roller, lose my footing once more.

"Stevie! Lookout!" Belfry shouted from somewhere above me.

The problem being, he shouted too late.

Head over heels, I plowed face first toward the rack housing crystals near the back room with a yelp of dismay. I managed to cover myself only in time to keep my face from smacking the edge of the shelving unit.

I lay in the pile of my rubble, a bit dazed as the dust settled, and Belfry swooped downward to land on my chest.

"Twinkle Toes?"

I began to sit up with a groan, my head aching. "Yes, Belfry?"

"If you can manage to do it without the effort resulting in an emergency brain transplant, turn around."

I blew at a strand of hair stuck to my mouth. "If I do what you ask, what will happen? Will the store fall into a sinkhole?"

"No, no. It's much, much worse."

His somber tone had me—and obviously my better judgment—sitting up straight.

As I took in the room behind the purple gauze material, my gasp echoed, the noise flying from my mouth, making me cringe and press my fingers to my lips.

I closed my eyes and gulped as Belfry climbed up my jacket and settled on my shoulder. "*Please,please,pleeease* tell me that isn't Madam Zoltar."

"I've only been saying as much for nigh on three hours now. Blimey, you Americans are slow."

Enter British Guy.

Jolly good show.

Chapter 3

"Belfry? Why can I hear but not see a British guy?"

"Winterbottom," a smooth voice whispered against my ear, sending a cool chill along my spine. I knew that chill. Oh yes, I did. British Guy was a real live ghost. That much of Belfry's story was true.

How could this be? I was a mortal now. No mortal I knew could *truly* talk to the dead. "Bottom who?"

I squinted and looked around the store, just as I did back in the good old days when a ghost made contact, hoping against hope I'd see him appear just the way ghosts always did in the past when they came to me for help. But there was nothing. No filmy, transparent glimmer of anything. Just a store trashed courtesy of yours truly.

What the heck was going on?

"I'm Winterbottom. The name's Winterbottom," the disembodied voice repeated.

I wasn't sure where to begin. With what I saw in the room behind the purple curtain, or the fact that I was hearing the voice of a ghost even though I technically shouldn't be able to hear anything from the afterlife.

I decided to attack the unclear first, before I sank my teeth into the obvious. "Okay, um, Bottom's Up, how can I hear you?"

"*Winter. Bottom,*" he enunciated, dry as a bone, sounding a lot like he'd stepped right out of an episode of *Game of Thrones*. "And it's a bit of a tale for the *X-Files*. A tale we don't have time to indulge in, but I'd be chuffed to pieces to share with you later. As you can see, we have far more pressing matters."

A warm breeze wafted past me and ruffled the gauzy material, revealing problem number two.

My eyes slammed shut and my fingers spread over my temple to pinch off the ensuing headache. "Madam Zoltar, I presume?"

"It is indeed. No need to check for a pulse, she's dead."

The desert my throat had become made it difficult to swallow. "What happened to her?"

"I don't know. That's why *you're* here. To help me figure it out."

"So all this trying to talk to Belfry was to get me to come here?"

"That wasn't the original intent."

"What was the original intent?" I asked.

"Forget that for now. As I was saying, you are, as they say here in the afterlife, the best in the biz. They also say you have a big heart, you're tenacious, you cry at Hallmark movies during Christmas, you're unbelievably gifted at finding bargain designer clothes from consignment shops and the like, you love a good mystery and are rather proficient at solving them, and you have a lovely shade of gray-blue eyes—of which I'd quite agree."

My cheeks flushed red. "That's very kind of them, and you. The problem is, I can't help you or anyone from the afterlife anymore."

"Mmm. I've heard. That's neither here nor there."

I stared up at the direction the voice came from and made a face. "No, that *is* here. Did the afterlife gossips fail to mention I'm not a witch anymore and all my medium powers are gone?"

"Yet, here you are, talking to me. They couldn't be gone entirely, because I truly *am* gone from this plane and still we communicate...um, sorry. What's your name?"

"The afterlife didn't tell you my name?"

"They're all quite vague here. As though you're some secret family recipe for Yorkshire pudding they aren't willing to share. They had the absolute audacity to tell me to get in line. Though, they did mention your very annoying familiar. Their words, not mine."

"Hey!" Belfry chirped. "I'm right here, you know. And it's Belfry, BTW. As in 'bats in the'."

I plucked Belfry up and tucked him against my chin, where he clung to the lapel on my jacket. "I'm Stevie, as in Nicks, the singer. Stevie Cartwright."

"The pleasure's all mine. Anyway, as you can see, we have a problem."

"Are you sure she's dead?"

"Positive."

When I'd assisted souls from the afterlife, they'd never sent me to help with a dead body. Still, I couldn't stop myself peeking around the corner of the purple material to assess the situation.

Madam Zoltar was flat out on the floor on her back in the mostly sparse space. Compared to the outer portion of the store, the back had no clutter at all. There was only a water cooler at the other end of the room in the right corner with some cone-shaped cups.

There was a wooden chair tipped over next to her, her body crumpled as though she'd slid from the seat she was sitting on at the round table and collapsed to the floor.

A purple tablecloth just touching the floor looked as though someone had yanked it half off the scarred table.

Madam Z must have grabbed it when she fell backward, which explained why the tarot cards were scattered over the top of the table and on the floor beside her still body.

She wore a turban made of some sort of white clingy material, with a big green jewel in the center, but a tuft of her graying hair poked out from beneath the edges by her neck. Her dress was flowing and multicolored, a caftan was how I'd classify it, with a matching jewel-encrusted neckline revealing her ample décolletage, and a scarf tied around her neck.

Gaudy rings graced almost every one of her fingers and in every color, with enormous costume gems. Yet her feet were bare, something I found curious. For someone who appreciated a little finery, I found it odd she didn't have matching kitten heels to complete her outfit, or at least a cute pair of functional flats.

That curiosity had my eyes swerving to her chubby feet. Ten toes were painted red and, in keeping with her love of jewelry, she had a toe ring on one middle toe.

But the ball of her right foot really caught my eye. There was a hole about two inches in size where her skin looked torn and missing, the edges of the wound almost charred. It was as though the spot on her foot had randomly exploded.

I'd call it a blister, but if that wound was a blister, I'd throw away the shoes that gave it to me.

My first instinct was to consider the obvious. A heart attack. After seeing the tablecloth she'd clearly dragged with her when she fell, it looked to me like she'd latched on to it in the throes of pain. Madam Z was an older woman, probably in her later sixties, her skin said as much. A heart attack made sense.

"Heart attack?" I finally asked out loud.

"I don't think so," Winterbottom replied, as if he had this all sewn up.

"Were you a medical examiner in your former life?"

"Um, nope. Guess again."

Planting my hands on my hips, I frowned into the empty store. "Then how do you know she didn't die of a heart attack or stroke? Did you see something?"

"No. Unfortunately, when I arrived just before I tried contacting you through Belfry this morning, Madame Zoltar was already dead."

Why was a legitimate ghost visiting a fake psychic? "You were here? Why?"

"We had business to attend."

"Could you be any more vague? You invited me to this party, Weatherwarning. I didn't crash it."

He chuckled, sort of low and slow and absolutely meant to be condescending. "Now you're just teasing me, Stevie Like-Nicks-the-Singer. Surely you're not that dense. I repeat, it's *Winterbottom*. And you make a fair statement. But it sounds as though we'll have to continue this conversation later. I believe I hear the dulcet tones of police sirens."

I froze, my eyes skimming the front of the store and the picture window, where the sign still blinked, looking for in-store cameras.

Ebenezer Falls was mostly crime-free as I remembered it, but that didn't mean Madam Z wasn't smart enough to protect herself on the off chance someone broke in. The last thing I needed was to end up on *America's Most Wanted.*

I raised my hand to cast a vanishing spell in case I'd been filmed and then I remembered, like a punch to the gut, I couldn't handle my problems with a spell and the flick of my hand anymore.

A thread of panic screamed through my veins, making my blood run cold. I'd had enough of being accused of something I didn't do in my witch life. I refused to start my human one with the local police as my guide.

Scooping Belfry from my collar, I located my purse on the countertop, where all my trouble began, and plopped him into it. "Okay, SummerButt or whatever your name is. I apologize in advance if I have that wrong, but I can't think straight when I'm in a panic. And this is me, officially in a panic. This looks bad. So, so bad. I'll call 9-1-1 once I'm safely out of here. They're going to take one look at this mess and think I had something to do with it!"

I'm not sure why I came to the conclusion the police would immediately think I'd killed Madam Zoltar. Maybe it was because I was still so freshly raw from my witch-slapping incident. Raw enough to know not everything is always as it seems.

I began picking my way through the debris of candles and crystals, wondering if I'd left muddy footprints anywhere with my galoshes. Didn't the forensic police always match footprints to shoes?

Of course they did. They did it all the time on *Castle.*

But there was no time for me to cover my tracks as the sirens grew closer.

The door to the store burst open, filling the interior with the sounds of the busy street outside. A short round man pushed his way through, almost tripping on some of the candles. "That's her!" he yelled, pointing at me.

There was a local police officer right behind him who eyed me critically, shoving the short man behind him in a protective gesture. "Police! Put your hands where I can see 'em!" He pointed what looked like the biggest gun in the history of guns right at me. "Chester! Stay behind me, would you?"

My hands flew upward in compliance; my purse, once in the crook of my arm, fell to my shoulder, unintentionally tossing poor Belfry around. No way was I giving anyone any guff. I watched YouTube. I knew what could happen if I got mouthy.

I fought a groan of distress as the officer approached me, his eyes narrowed and suspicious, as if he'd just caught Hoffa in the middle of a mob kill.

"Let me explain," I began, keeping my tone even and, above all, calm while I forced myself to look into his dark brown eyes.

If I were going to explain, I'd do it right to his handsome face like someone who was telling the truth.

"That's her!" the round senior with suspenders and a plaid green-flannel shirt chirped, as though he'd just identified Bigfoot. "Saw her comin' in here about fifteen minutes ago then heard all the ruckus from my son's coffee shop next door. Called you boys right up."

I swallowed the lump in my throat. "That's true, Officer. The gentleman's absolutely right. It was about fifteen minutes ago. I was just…"

Just what? What could I possibly tell them? I came in to investigate the voice my bat familiar heard calling to him from the afterlife? And as a point of interest, he's a ghost with a British accent and his name's SpringLoaded—or something fancy and pretentious.

Ugh! When I got my hands on British Guy, I was going to knock him right into the next plane!

Gathering myself, I decided I had to be very careful about what I said and how I said it. "I just came in to look around. I'm recently back in Ebenezer Falls after being gone for a decade or so, and there are so many new things to see—"

"Then why in tarnation did it sound like a herd of elephants was doin' the fandango in here?" the sweet-looking senior asked. "These walls are thin, lady. You were in here roughin' up my Tina, that's what you were doing!"

I found it hard to hide my surprise as I looked into this man's blue eyes, so alive with anguish. "Who's Tina?"

Winterbottom's rich, sophisticated voice grazed my ear. "That's Madam Zoltar's real name. Tina Marie Martoni. And this little chap with the suspenders and sharp eyes? He's Chester Sherwood. Seventy-two, and a spry old goat. His son runs and owns the coffee shop next door."

I rolled my shoulder to dislodge Winterbottom from my ear. If there was anything I was skilled at, it was ignoring clingy ghosts who wanted to talk when I was in the middle of something.

"May I put my hands down now, Officer? I think my fingers are numb."

But Chester began hopping around in protest, the tuft of white hair on his balding head bouncing in time with his feet. "She was in here up to no good! Tell her to keep her hands in the air 'til her fingers fall off!"

Aw. That was kinda mean. I sent big pleading eyes to the officer, averting my gaze away from Chester The Heckler.

The officer lowered his gun and holstered it when his backup arrived, but he pointed a warning finger at me. "You can put your hands down, but you stay where we can see you." Then he turned to his partner, a reed-thin, sandy-blond man who had to be at least six-three. "Keep an eye on her, Gorton, while I take a look around. She was here in the middle of all this when I got to the scene."

"Wait!" I yelped a warning without even thinking. "Madam Zoltar's..." I looked to Chester, who had called her "his" Tina, leading me to believe there might be some kind of romantic attachment, so I wanted to tread delicately. I'd hate it if I blurted out in a careless manner that she'd left this world.

So I inched my way over to the first officer on the scene, and caught his name badge. Dropping my voice to a whisper, I leaned into him. "Um, Officer Nelson? Madam Zoltar is dead."

Chester was becoming more agitated by the second. He gripped the tall officer, his fingers sinking into the policeman's forearm, his lips thinning into a line. "What are you whisperin' about over there, girlie! What did you do to my Tina?"

Officer Nelson planted his hands on slender hips. "And how do you know she's departed, Miss—"

I stuck my hand out between us, cutting off his words. "Cartwright. Stevie Cartwright. I know because I saw her. If you'll just let me explain—"

He gave me a sharp gaze that said shut it and firmly ignored my hand, but his spoken instruction was polite. "If you'll just wait here, Miss Cartwright, I'll take a look."

As Officer Nelson climbed over the carnage of my klutziness, I shoved my unshaken hand back to my side and held my breath.

From this distance, I saw him kneel down next to Madam Zoltar, pressing his fingers to her wrist. Then he spoke softly into the radio at his shoulder, obviously alerting headquarters there was no rush.

It was then the sorrow of a soul passing over hit me in waves of remorse, arcing over my initial shock. Madam Zoltar had probably been someone's mother, sister, daughter, friend. I hoped wherever she'd landed on the other side, she was happy.

I said a small prayer to that effect while Officer Nelson assessed me again with a critical pair of brown eyes, his tight jaw and clean good looks hard to ignore. He struck me as the kind of man who made hospital corners on his bed and devoutly avoided anything chaotic.

But it appeared as though he wouldn't be able to avoid chaos today. As passersby and probably other shop owners began to gather at the window and the entry to the store, more police arrived.

Was Madam Zoltar important to the community in a way other than her work? Or were these rubberneckers just a bunch of ambulance chasers?

"Nana Tina?" someone from the back of the forming crowd called, followed by a pale hand waving from the street.

All heads swiveled to see where the cry had come from before a young woman barreled through the gawkers.

Her eyes were wide and green, her hair dyed so red, under the dim light of the store it looked almost pink. The cut was shaggy and unkempt, worn jagged and spiky around her heart-shaped face. She had on as much jewelry as her nana, but she wore most of it in the way of piercings in her eyebrows and nose.

The slouch of her loose jeans rolled at her ankles, a pair of navy-blue Keds and a neon-green hoodie all said she was quite young.

"*Nana Tina?*" she cried out again, her eyes taking in the mess on the floor. Then she looked to Officer Nelson. "Where is my nana?"

I knew what was coming, and the very thought made me hurt for this young woman.

Officer Nelson's wide shoulders slumped for only a moment before he squared them and stepped in her path, blocking her from the back room. "May I ask who you are?"

Anxiety began to take over, that much was clear from her tone and the way she attempted to get around him. "I'm Liza Martoni. I'm Tina, er, Madam Zoltar's granddaughter. Now where is she? What happened? Was she robbed?" Tears stemming from obvious fear were beginning to form in the corners of her eyes, threatening to spill from her round orbs.

Officer Nelson placed a broad hand on Liza's shoulder, and though he towered over her, he still managed to keep his voice gentle. "I'd afraid she's gone, Miss Martoni. I'm very sorry for your loss."

"Gone?" Liza wailed, collapsing against the glass counter. "What happened?"

"That's what we're here to try to find out. Please, let Officer Gorton take you outside so we can investigate thoroughly." Officer Nelson swept a hand toward the door, but Liza began to sob, clinging to him.

"Why do you have to investigate? What's to investigate? She's my nana. I have a right to know! Tell me what happened!" she begged, twisting my heart.

I couldn't take it anymore. Someone had to comfort her. I normally only dealt with people after they were gone. I usually didn't see the sorrow and grief. I had to at least reach out and offer her some consolation, something other than the unsympathetic eyes of Officer Nelson, who appeared desperately uncomfortable.

Putting my hand on Liza's arm, I squeezed. "Why don't you let the police do what they have to and come outside with me, Liza? I'll wait with you." I wasn't supposed to leave Officer Gorton's sight, but I didn't care if it got me into trouble. Liza shouldn't have to see this.

Instantly, her round eyes melted into a puddle of more tears when she took my hand. "I can't believe this happened," she sobbed. "I just saw her yesterday. She was fine."

I squeezed her hand and patted her arm, keeping my body in front of hers so she wouldn't see Madam Zoltar's still body. "I'm so sorry, Liza. Can I get you something? A water, maybe? Coffee? What's your pleasure? My treat."

She shook her head and sniffed, her spiky hair ruffling. "No...no, thank you. I just want to know what's going on. I *need* to know what's going on."

It was almost as if she didn't fully understand that no one *knew* what was going on. "They don't know just yet, Liza. That's why we have to let the police do their job." I tried inching her toward the door, and away from the gruesome figure of her nana lying on the floor, but she wasn't budging.

"How does a perfectly healthy sixty-eight-year-old woman die suddenly?"

"So your nana was in good health?"

"She was an ox!" Liza spat, anger now clearly replacing her grief. "She'd just been to the doctor and left with a clean bill of health. And that's why I want to know what happened. Because this doesn't make any sense!"

I grasped at straws when I offered, "Maybe it was an intruder? A theft of some kind?"

Though that didn't make a lot of sense, even to me. Her foot had an injury I wasn't qualified to diagnose, but an intruder made no sense. Nothing had been disturbed.

Liza finally looked up at me, but behind those big watery eyes was something. Something I couldn't put my finger on.

Her frantic eyes went to the seemingly untouched register. "Then why wasn't anything taken from the cash register? Was something stolen? Because it sure doesn't look like it. Plus, there's an alarm she wears around her neck. It's a necklace, small chain, a pendant with a sapphire-blue jewel in it she can press discreetly and it silently signals a place called Senior Alert. We made her get one when she wouldn't give up the store because we worried about her and the late hours she kept just to keep this place running. She hated wearing it. She wouldn't have had to wear it at all if she didn't need the money her readings brought to supplement her income because the government's cheap idea of a pension wasn't enough for a *cat* to live on!"

Funny, I didn't remember a necklace around her throat. You'd think for all the jewelry Madam Zoltar wore, she wouldn't forget something so important. I wanted to ask Liza more questions, despite the fact that I had no idea what I was doing. Something wasn't sitting well with me—or right—or whatever.

I smiled and attempted another push toward the door, hoping I could get her safely through the crowd. "So she was a hard worker, your nana Tina? Come and tell me all about her, would you? She sounds so interesting. I mean, how many people are lucky enough to have a psychic medium in the family? Let's grab some coffee. There's a coffee cafe just next door, I hear. It's new to me because I've been away since I graduated high school and I'm dying to try it."

Officer Nelson hitched his jaw in the direction of his partner Gorton, stepping in front of us. "I'm afraid you won't be able to do that, Miss Cartwright."

My eyes flew to his sharply constructed face as my pulse raced. "Why's that?"

A voice from behind me answered my question in a cordial tone. "Because you're coming to the station for questioning, Miss Cartwright."

Liza promptly dropped my hand, her mouth falling open. "Oh my God! Was it *you?* Did you hurt her?"

Everyone at the door went silent and looked at me with the glare of a thousand fiery suns.

Oh, seven hells.

Officer Nelson stepped in before I could protest, keeping Liza from me and somehow redirecting her to another officer who'd arrived on the scene.

My stomach sank. I didn't need this kind of trouble so early on in my return to Ebenezer Falls. It was all I could do not to scream right then and there.

So for sure, when I got my hands on Winterbutt, he was a dead ghost walking.

For. Sure.

Chapter 4

Swallowing around the thick lump in my throat, I widened my stance. "Questioning? *For what?*" I shouted in disbelief, whipping around to catch my first glimpse of the newest person to enter the fray.

The latest man dressed in blue from Ebenezer Falls's finest was wide like a linebacker, solid and imposing, but for his openly cheerful face, which was round and pleasant, with ruddy cheeks and lively eyes, all topped with shortly cropped muddy-brown hair. He stopped and gaped at me.

"Stevie Cartwright, is that *you?* Wow, you look just like you did back in school. Haven't changed a bit. Well, except you nixed the black lipstick and all that eye makeup you used to wear. Remember me? It's Sandwich! We graduated together, class of 2001. Holy spitballs, long time no see!" He grinned at me, his eyes swallowed up by his round cheeks.

Nelson cleared his throat and put on his "I'm in charge" face, meaning, quit passing pleasantries with the suspect. "Officer Paddington. Please take Miss Cartwright to the station."

Sandwich Paddington, who I was still trying to place, tipped his hat at Nelson, his pleasant face going crimson. "Oh yeah. Right. Right. Sorry, Stevie. It's my job."

As Sandwich went for my arm to escort me out, I took a step back. "Hold up! Am I being arrested?"

Officer Nelson gave me the policeman's glare of authority. "Not unless you *make* me arrest you. We'd just like to ask you some questions in a more formal setting about what happened here, Miss Cartwright. If you're not agreeable, I can certainly cuff you."

Shaking my head, I held my hands up. The last thing I needed to do was create a scene in front of the people who would be my neighbors. "That won't be necessary. I'm happy to answer any questions you have."

With that, I made my way through the burgeoning crowd, past Chester, who growled at me and snapped his teeth, and out toward the police car, still trying to figure out who Sandwich was.

I'd been cautious about getting too close to anyone during high school. I could do things no one else could—like talk to the dead—and I was still learning how to manage it when I grew into my teens. No one in Ebenezer Falls knew I was a witch, and at that very crucial time in my life, when I was awkward and my self-esteem was at its lowest, I'd put myself in self-imposed isolation.

As we made our way to the curb, the eyes of Ebenezer Falls were on me. Burning a hole into my back, people whispering behind their hands.

I was about to make my way to the passenger door when Sandwich scuffled behind me and gripped my elbow. "Sorry, Stevie. I have to put you in the backseat."

There was a groan from the interior of my purse I had no choice but to ignore as I got in the backseat, crossing my arms over my chest.

"You want me to put the sirens on?" Sandwich asked, his face smiling at me from the rearview mirror.

"To announce I'm being questioned in the death of Madam Zoltar?"

His face went bright red. "Aw, shoot. I wasn't thinking about that. I was just thinking people always ask because they think it's kinda cool. Sorry."

I managed a smile. "It's okay, Sandwich. Under any other circumstances, I'd be all for it. So here's a question maybe you can answer. *Am* I under suspicion in the death of Madam Zoltar?"

His wide shoulders bumped upward. "I dunno. Nelson just called for backup and when I got there, Gorton said Nelson's orders were to bring you in for questioning and a statement. It's standard procedure. That much I can tell ya."

That made me feel a little better, but not by a lot.

As rain battered the windshield of the cruiser while we whisked through the streets of Ebenezer Falls, I tried to place his face, but failed miserably. "So you say we graduated together?"

While I mostly kept to myself in my high school days, it wasn't only due to the fact that I was a witch, but also because I did broody-Goth-rejected-from-society like a champ. I saw it on a show I'd watched and decided I had no real identity. Nothing people would remember me for. Like a signature label that said, "Hey, remember Stevie Cartwright? She always used to wear black clothes and matching black lipstick and we all thought she was part of a satanic cult?"

I thought it made me dark and mysterious, when I suppose it just made me look like a good portion of Seattle's youth.

"Yep. We were in the same English class our senior year. Remember Mr. Stowe?"

"A trip down memory lane. How quaint," Winterbottom muttered in my ear.

I ignored him, and the fact that he was a traveling ghost, unfettered by the usual hurdles ghosts encounter. Like moving from place to place without some object to tether them. I also continued to ignore the fact that he could communicate with me when my medium abilities were long gone.

Or were they? I was afraid to get my hopes up. So I squashed them like an annoying fly, hovering over a plate of watermelon.

No way was I going to get all juiced just to find out this was some crazy fluke, or worse, start hoping maybe I'd retained some of my powers. I couldn't be crushed like that twice in a lifetime.

"Hah!" I barked. "Do I remember Mr. Stowe?" I scrunched up my face and made a sour expression, puffing out my chest. "These are classics we're reading, children! This is Shakespeare and Theroux. Just because they don't use words like 'dis' and 'da-bomb' doesn't mean they can't be equally as interesting!"

Sandwich howled a laugh. "That was Mr. Stowe all right."

Even racking my brain, I still couldn't remember Sandwich. "I can't believe I don't remember you."

"Well, if I'm honest, I didn't show up near as much as I shoulda. But I straightened out pretty good. And my real name's Lyn. Lyn Paddington. They called me Sandwich because someone once dared me to eat a sardine sandwich with mayo and sweet pickles in the cafeteria."

That's when it hit me. "Oh! I do remember! You threw up on Principal Fellows at assembly in the auditorium!"

A groan whispered in my ear, giving me a rash of goose bumps along my arms. "Ah. You Americans. You're so well educated—or maybe a more apt word is refined. Is it any wonder you have people the likes of The K—"

"Shh!" I ordered, only to realize Sandwich was looking at me with curious eyes. So I faked a loud sneeze. "Sorry. I think I'm catching a cold. So you threw up on Principal Fellows."

"Yep. That was me. Lost my cookies all over the front row, too. Had the nickname ever since. So what brings you back to Ebenezer Falls, Stevie? Heard you moved to New York for a little while. Then I think we lost track of ya come reunion time."

How did I explain this? A crooked council member and a witch-slapping to beat all slaps is what had me here, tail between my legs. My life in ruins, maybe?

I sighed. Rather than tell him the truth, I put my Stevie spin on my tale of woe. "I missed home, I guess. You know, you get to a certain age and you start to hanker for the things that once brought you comfort. Familiar things, I suppose."

His glance told me he wasn't quite sure what I meant. Probably because Sandwich had never left Ebenezer Falls. "Heard your mom moved to Rome. That's pretty exciting."

Yep. With warlock husband number five, who'd advised her to stay out of the mess I was in for fear the council would exact some kind of retribution. Bart the warlock was all about playing by the council rules, and my mother, Dita, was happy to oblige, seeing as Bart paid all the bills for their posh villa and cruises to Saint Tropez.

"She did. She seems very happy there."

Sandwich pulled to a stop in front of the police station, right across the street from the docks where various boats were tied up along the sides of the pier, bobbing in the choppy waters of February.

The police station hadn't changed much. Not that I spent any amount of time here when I was a kid. I'd been on a tour once during a scared-straight seminar that was all the rage when we were in high school.

Mostly, the lesson was don't end up like Old Man Cletus, who drank a little at this old bar where fishermen hung out and ended up in the drunk tank from time to time. He was the best Ebenezer Falls had to offer in the way of hardened criminals, and the program scared absolutely no one straight.

The brick structure still lacked the intimidation factor. In fact, it looked more like a long, flat house, with its arched windows and winding cobblestone pathway lined with short box-hedges.

Sandwich put his hands on the steering wheel and caught my gaze from the rearview mirror. "We're here."

I blew out a breath and waited for him to open the door before I slid out and followed him across the parking lot and toward the glass front door. "Hey, thanks, Sandwich. It's been fun remembering old times."

Pulling at the door, he drove his free hand inside his pocket, his round cheeks turning red at their crests. "Maybe you could just call me Lyn inside around the other guys? Professional and all."

Winterbottom snarfed a laugh in my ear. "This from the man who vomited his dare sandwich all over your principal. The ultimate professional really does exist."

I bit my tongue. Winterbottom and whatever his problem was would have to wait.

As I let Sandwich, er, Lyn guide me to the front desk, I tried to maintain my cool. I was innocent of any wrongdoing. And I'd better be good at proving it because I couldn't afford a taco, let alone a lawyer.

***

An hour later and I was a free woman, with the warning I shouldn't leave town just yet. I waved to Sandwich and a couple of other people I'd become reacquainted with during the course of my questioning as I made my way out of the police station, fighting the urge to stick my tongue out at Officer Nelson and yell something childish like, "Neener, neener, neener! You blew any future appearances on *To Catch A Killer*."

Speaking of killers, I had to wonder what led them to believe Madam Zoltar had been killed—or if they even thought she'd been murdered at all. I had, after all, been the only living person to find Madam Zoltar. It made sense they'd want to ask me questions about what I'd witnessed, but they could have asked me those questions at her store.

Maybe this wasn't a murder investigation at all. Maybe it was nothing more than an inquiry and I was jumping to conclusions. I'd let too much television crime drama and that rigid Officer Nelson of the granite jaw and imposing stance get up in my head.

One narrow-eyed gaze from him, and I almost felt like I *had* committed a crime.

"Stevieeee!" Belfry sounded on the verge of death.

But I wasn't done being angry with him for dragging me into Madam Zoltar's. I'd had a gut feeling I ignored and now I was involved in something I wanted nothing to do with.

"I'm going to kill you."

"Fair enough, but could you do it after you feed me? I'm bottom of the barrel here."

I had to give it to him, he'd stayed quiet as a mouse all while they'd asked me about finding Madam Z and how the store had been torn apart. But part of that was most certainly guilt. I knew quiet remorse from Belfry, even if I couldn't exactly feel his vibration of life thrumming through my veins anymore.

"I told you we shouldn't go in, Bel. Why don't you ever listen?"

"Oh, c'mon. Be fair. Have you heard Mr. Accent? Who can resist a guy who sounds like Benedict Cumberbatch and Jon Snow all in one tally-ho?"

"Yeah. Who can resist an accent from over the pond, Stevie?"

My eyes rolled. "You're still here? I'll tell you who. Me. That's who. I didn't resist and now look. I'm a suspect in a murder investigation."

"That's very dramatic, Stevie. They're not calling it murder yet, but they will be. Or should I say, they should be—and you're going to help me prove it."

I stopped walking and scooted into an alleyway so no one would see what looked like me essentially talking to myself. "Listen up, Winterbourne—"

"You're just being facetious now, Stevie," he teased. "It's Winterbottom and you know it. But most everyone calls me Win. That'll do for now."

I narrowed my eyes at the empty space in front of me. "Oh, will it? Thanks for giving me permission, *Win*. Which, by the by, is the least of what I want to call you. You knew I was going in there blind. You knew I'm not a witch anymore. That I can't defend myself the way I used to. Under normal circumstances, I'd have snapped my fingers and we'd have been out of there in a puff of my signature smoke and no one would have ever been the wiser."

"How was I to know you'd actually show up? I spent a bloody torturous hour trying to get through to Belfry here, and even then he only caught bits and pieces of what I was attempting to communicate. But you did show up, Stevie. That means the experiment worked and we were fated to meet."

"*The experiment?*"

47

"A very long, exceptionally harrowing story from my training days I'll share at a later date. For now, don't you find it incredible I'm able to communicate with *you*, someone with no powers, from the grave no less? It's damn well fantastic."

Yeah, yeah. It was a fantastic way to have the rug yanked out from under me. When I wasn't under suspicion for Madam Z's death anymore, I'd investigate further. Until then, no hope-dashing. If nothing else, his back story about an experiment was fascinating and deserved some attention.

"Your training days?" Gah. My endless curiosity always brought trouble.

I imagined Win waving his hands dismissively to pooh-pooh me. "Never mind that now. We have things we must accomplish. The first of which is finding you a place to live."

Had he been listening in on my conversations? "How do you know I don't have a place to live?"

"Hah. The afterlife is rich with chatter about you, Stevie. How do you think I found you in the first place? It's taken me a month to get in touch with you as it is."

That pang of longing for my old life struck me hard. So hard, I leaned back against the brick wall in the alley.

Clearly it showed.

"Chin up, Stevie. We have no time for self-pity today. We have shelter to find and a murderer to catch."

"No. I have a long overdue lunch to eat and a motel to get back to."

"I'll buy you lunch if you'll hear me out," Win tempted with a voice low and deep.

"With what, your ghostly rupees?"

"Fine then. I can't buy it right this moment, but rest assured, I'll buy you all the lunch your witchless heart desires if you'll just hear my story."

This was crazy. But it wasn't the craziest thing I'd ever done. It had to be my lower-than-low blood sugar that made me agree. I stood up straight and squared my shoulders. "Okay, tell me your story."

"Not here." He sounded offended.

"What's wrong with here?"

"Simply everything," he drawled. "Come with me and we'll get your lunch. You can eat it while we discuss the matter at hand."

I nodded my head, too hungry to argue, exiting the alleyway and heading toward the taco food truck. My stomach cheered my decision.

I stopped at the corner where Madam Zoltar's store was located, glad to see the crowd had dispersed. There was official yellow police tape barring the door, and a man dressed in a long tan trench coat—a Burberry, if I was seeing right—and plastic on his shoes, ducked under the tape.

He looked pretty official, leading me to believe maybe they'd brought in some detectives. I wasn't sure if I felt relieved or sadder than I had been before. I couldn't stop thinking about Liza and her anguish. I hated that she thought I'd set out to comfort her to cover something as treacherous as murder.

But I forced that from my mind and inhaled a deep, relieved breath. Tacos, here I come.

I began to make a beeline toward the taco truck when my ghost grunted his disapproval. "Ick. Must you?" Winterbottom asked with plain distaste.

"Must I what?"

"Eat tacos?"

"Right?" Belfry chimed in. "I'm always telling her she has the taste buds of a twelve-year-old trucker."

He made it sound like I was eating toxic waste straight from the hazardous barrel with a spork. "I promise, next lunch I'll eat at the Dom Pérignon and Caviar Made with the Tears of a Dutch Virgin truck. But for now, tacos are all I can fit into my rapidly dwindling budget. Or didn't the afterlife gossips tell you that where my savings account once resided now lives an old troll and a tumbleweed?"

"They didn't. But they did tell me you had an incredibly delightful sense of humor. I'll definitely give you cheeky."

"Ooo. Talk dirty to me," I joked, crossing the street.

"I beg your pardon?"

"Forget it. It's a crass American joke form an even crasser American ex-witch. Now back off and let me get my tacos made from recycled lettuce and the maw of dandelion."

"Is this my cue to let you have a moment to yourself?"

My head bounced up and down as I gave my eye of the tiger to the taco truck with its candy-striped awning and fun dancing tacos wearing sombreros hand painted on the side. "It's your cue to let me wrestle with some mystery meat and extra cheese in peace."

"Very well. Peace you shall have."

The cool/warm encompassing me, a strange yet indefinable sensation I'd felt as I talked to Win, evaporated, meaning he'd gone back to the plane he was from to let me think.

Waving to my favorite taco vendor, I skipped to the window of his truck with one thought in mind—eating. I met Tito two days after I'd arrived back in Ebenezer Falls, and we'd been making beautiful music in my mouth together since.

I loved his thick Spanish accent, his adorable attempts at broken English—which he had once confided he practiced often in order to get his permanent visa here in the US—his jovial smile, his generous helpings that kept me full enough to sometimes skip dinner…a blessing on my wallet.

Thankfully, he was sans his usual long line of hungry lunch crowd. Peering up at him, I smiled.

And Tito slammed the window shut in my face with a scowl.

I looked at the hours on his sign and frowned. It was only three and it said he was open until ten. Standing on my tiptoes, I rapped on the window. "Hey, Tito! You're supposed to be open until ten. I get bankers' hours, but even bankers don't call it a day at three."

Nothing but silence and the sounds of the street greeted my ears.

So I knocked again. "Tito?"

There was a low mumble of something, something I couldn't distinguish. I leaned in closer, my calf muscles straining, and then I saw the top of Tito's head, his thick, dark hair just cresting the window before falling away from my limited line of vision.

And now I was getting angry. "Hey! I know you're in there. I can see you! What's the world come to if a starving woman can't get a taco at three in the afternoon when closing time isn't until ten, Tito?"

And then the vendor appeared at the window, pointing his chubby finger at me in accusation. "We don' serve murderers!"

No *bueno*.

Chapter 5

Murderer. I'd been branded a murderer. By a taco vendor, no less. Boy, did that cut deep.

I plucked at my soggy drive-thru burger, dropping an equally soggy French fry into my mouth as Belfry munched on his apple slice in my purse, and Win reassured me one more time he would pay me back for the cab fare to wherever this 711 Samantha Lane was located.

"I promise you," he said. "You'll have all the money you need if you'll just indulge me."

I'd waved him out of my ear. "Reign in the sunshine. Still a little raw here, Win."

After that, the ride was mostly silent. Me sitting shiva at my accused murderer pity-party, Win humming some odd tune I didn't know.

When we pulled up to the address he'd given me, I realized my wallowing had kept me from paying attention to my surroundings. How had we gotten out here to the bluff?

Closing my eyes, I inhaled the scent of the Sound. I loved this place. I loved the stretch of a quarter mile of nothing but trees and the occasional break in them where the mountains peeked through. I'd come here hundreds of times during my childhood, taking the two-mile bike ride from the outskirts of Ebenezer Falls right here to almost the end of our small town.

Everyone always thought it was spooky out here, but I was a witch who talked to the dead. Naturally, not a lot spooked me. I couldn't remember anyone ever living in the house Win claimed was his, but I did remember it hadn't looked quite so haunted Victorian as it did today.

As I took in the decaying house at the top of the cliff, I groaned. This was what all the chatty buildup had been about? All the, "Just wait, Stevie, it's smashing. You're going to love it. It's right on a cliff overlooking the Sound. Private, sprawling, plenty of room for Belfry to fly" had been over this?

This? It was a monstrosity. A falling-apart-at-the-seams, crumbling-in-almost-every-corner monstrosity.

But I held my tongue. Mostly because I was still too angry with Win for ruining my torrid affair with my favorite taco truck to speak, and it didn't really matter if I was angry here or back in my hotel room.

I paid the driver and slid out, bracing myself for the wind and rain that would surely pummel my face. Thankfully, I still had my galoshes on. I'd need them if I had any hope of climbing the steep, muddy incline leading to the crooked front porch.

The concrete stairs had caved inward at some point, cracked and certainly too dangerous to walk on. Not to mention, a good deal of the wrought iron railings were missing, too.

I stopped when we were almost to the top, gasping for breath, and that was when I got a close-up glimpse of the underside of the porch steps, rotting away as we stood there.

The wind picked up, pushing me forward so hard, I had to steady myself. "Is it safe?"

"Don't be ridiculous. Would I take you anywhere that wasn't safe?"

"Would you take me somewhere there's been a murder? I think the answer is yes. So forgive me if I question your definition of safe."

His sigh rasped in my ear, going in one and out the other. "How long will you grudge, Stevie?"

"For as long as I'm connected to Madam Zoltar's suspicious death, and probably long after that. So in non-ghost speak—*forever*."

"Forever's a long time, now hurry along. We have things to discuss."

I plowed up the remaining bit of hill and hit the front porch steps with a wince, my mind still so full of the images of today. Liza's raw grief. Mr. Sherwood's face when he accused me of hurting "his Tina."

And that Senior Alert necklace Liza made mention of that wasn't around Madam Zoltar's neck or anywhere near her fallen body. Maybe I'd just missed it, but it was poking at me something fierce. I didn't want to believe she'd been murdered, but my gut said something quite different.

As I climbed the steps, I wondered if they'd even hold my weight. I was no size two. I wasn't even a size eight. And they looked mighty weak. I'd had a hella bad day. Adding falling through some rotting stairs to my death to the roster would send me right over the edge.

I stepped onto the porch with great care and took my first look around. The stained-glass door with a beautiful pattern of greens, blues and maroon I couldn't make sense of was warped, but could be quite lovely refinished and re-stained. It was wide and thick, handcrafted rather than bought at a local box store.

The sprawling porch, flanked by four pillars, wrapped around each side of the three-story house. Planks of wood popped up, the boards were loose and splintered, the paint peeling everywhere. An enormous hole by one of the thick pillars looked like someone had dropped a heavy ball through it.

"The key's under the mat."

Winterbottom's statement made me wonder how long he'd owned this dump. I stooped, lifting up the disintegrating, soggy mat covered in slimy leaves, and found a shiny brass key. Pushing it into the keyhole, I turned it—with no luck.

"It's jammed. Bummer. Guess I'll have to pay for another cab ride home you can put on your final bill. Too bad, so sad."

"Did you always give up this easily when you were a witch? Lift the handle and turn."

With a defeated sigh, I did as instructed. Popping the door open, I squinted and scanned the gigantic square entryway as my eyes adjusted.

Someone had knocked the wall out between the parlor and the entry. I say "knocked it out" because it literally looked as though someone had plowed through it with their body. The hole was jagged and rough, the sheetrock crumbled and littering the floor.

I gave a good look around the place, my eyes going to the staircase on my left, winding upward to the second floor where window upon window lined the head of the steps.

If you looked directly across the entryway and down the short hall, there was a room I guessed was a kitchen, but I couldn't see much other than more windows and junk. All manner of fast-food cartons and pizza boxes, crushed beer and soda cans were strewn from one end of the entry to the next. It was filthy and smelled like desperation and cat urine.

"So, what do you think?" Win asked, as though he were proudly asking me to rate on a scale of one to ten how cute his newborn baby was.

"Who's your decorator, Marilyn Manson?"

"Oh, it's all fun and games until you find out I actually know a Manson. Charlie, to be precise. Isn't that right, Stevie Like-Nicks-the-Singer?"

Laughter gurgled from my throat against my will. I'd give Mr. British Guy this, he could make with the funny.

But how peculiar he should mention knowing one of America's most controversial serial killers. What had been Winterbottom's profession before he'd died? My guess was prison guard.

My eyebrow rose as I stepped over a torn bag of Funyuns and an empty six-pack of Dr. Pepper. "You know Charles Manson?"

"Well, I don't *know him* know him. We don't lunch or anything. I met him. Once. I interviewed him about another case that didn't involve him, but was similar to his portfolio of crimes."

A case? Curioser and curioser.

"Okay, so did his cellmate help you decorate this place?" I asked, my fingers trailing over the thick covering of dust on a three-legged end table by the side of the stairs.

"They were beyond helpful in my quest to make sure the paint peeled in all the right places."

I glanced around again at the wall that looked as though someone had tried to scratch their way out of the parlor from behind the sheetrock and nodded. "Tell him job well done. He's an overachiever."

Winterbottom's chuckle, deep and rich, swirled in my ears, sweeping over the room. "And it's all yours."

Say what now?

I kept my surprise on the inside, but I gripped the wobbly square finial on the staircase banister to steady myself.

"It's what?"

"All yours, if you'll have it."

I held up a hand, setting my purse on the warped hardwood floor so if he chose, Belfry could poke his head out when he was done napping. "I think I need some clarity. Who were you when you were alive and how can you give me an entire house?"

There was a pause, as though he was gathering steam to prepare me for something heinous. It hadn't occurred to me up to this point, but what if he was a bad guy? What if he was some crappy shyster of a real estate developer who stole from seniors, or a Bernie Madoff type dude?

"Are you ready for this?"

"Do you really think anything you tell me can move the register on my surprise meter any higher after the events of today? Divulge or I go back to my hotel room."

"I was a spy."

My head cocked to the right while his words nested in my brain. "A spy as in private investigator, Inspector Clouseau…or a spy like the spy in the show *Alias*?"

"Oh, definitely an *Alias*-caliber spy. Sydney's my hero."

Visions of Sydney Bristow danced through my head. Images of this faceless man, with his educated, succinct words and light disdain, wearing a wig for a disguise, swiftly followed.

"You're very quiet, Stevie."

I gnawed on the inside of my cheek. While intrigued, I was far from sold.

"Well, here's the thing. You could tell me you were the King of Prussia and I'd have no way to prove you weren't, right? I can't see ghosts anymore, so visible identification is out. Do you have a driver's license or something? Some kind of ID?"

"I have ten. Or I *had* ten. I also had ten matching passports, a killer Aston Martin and lots of zeros at the end of the numbers in my various bank accounts. Of course, that was before I was dead. Who knows what's happened to my locker back in London by now though. Oh, and the King of Prussia looks nothing like me. His name was Wilhelm, as a point of reference."

Ignoring his glib history lesson, I plowed ahead. "So your home base was in London?"

"It was," he purred. "Rather a command central, if you will. A place where all good spies go home to rest after they've finished a grueling mission wherein one is shot at from a helicopter while hanging by the skids."

I fought a roll of my eyes. Win was coming off like the crackpots on the Internet who wove tales of great heroism when in real life they were plumbers. Everyone was a superstar until you could prove otherwise.

"Sounds like the stuff *Mission Impossible* movies are made of."

"I'm better looking than Cruise," he said on a chuckle.

Crossing my arms over my chest, I asked, "So, is that how you died? Were you shot while hanging on to the skids of a helicopter?"

"The time will come when I tell you how I died. For now, just know I'm pretty dead."

I found it almost laughable he thought I was supposed to just accept his explanation because he said I should. I added arrogant to my list of rapidly growing Winterbottom characteristics.

But I wasn't letting him off so easy. That he expected me to simply take his word for it was, in another word, insane.

Planting my hand on my hip, I lifted my chin and gave him some of his arrogance right back. "Can I call someone at spy command central and ask about you? Get references?"

"You could, but no one would answer your questions. That's why I was called a spy, Stevie. Secrets and lies are heartily encouraged."

Of course they were. "Again, I'll remind you, you can pretend to be whoever you want to be and I won't know any different."

"Would you like an afterlife reference? Someone who goes by the name Digby Reynolds?"

That stopped me cold. Digby had died a particularly untimely death back in Texas. While witches and warlocks were immortal, if taken by surprise, we can still end up really dead.

Digby died when an oak tree in the center of Paris was split by lightning and fell on him. His cat, Maynard, was the only family he had, and Digby came to me, asking that I rehome him.

"Okay, ask Digby what his cat's name was?"

There was a pause and then Winterbottom's voice echoed in my ear. "Maynard. A tabby you were kind enough to find a new home for with a woman named Greta, who runs some sort of halfway house for witches in Paris, Texas, with a friend of yours named Winnie Yagamowitz."

Hearing Winnie's name made me smile. I missed Winnie and her daughter Lola.

Okay, so he could talk to some of the people I've helped. That proved nothing. "Do me a favor?"

"Anything."

"Tell Digby to stop waffling and make a decision. He passed well over eight months ago. It's time to choose a path to the light, or accept the afterlife plane he's on as his eternity."

"He stuck his tongue out at you."

I chuckled. That definitely sounded like Digby. Yet, it still didn't change much. "So you can talk to people on the other side. I didn't *doubt* you were on the other side. That still doesn't prove you were who you say you were."

"But it does prove I know some of the ghosts you were in contact with. You came so highly recommended. I thought you'd be thrilled to your knickers to help me."

"Ghosts are a chatty lot. If you're on the plane where people who are undecided land, they love to gab in order to put off making a choice. You might be a spy, but I know ghosts. And my knickers have skeptical written all over them. How do I know you're not setting me up?"

"We're getting nowhere fast."

"Whose fault is that, Spy Guy?"

"Forget my prior profession, Stevie, and focus on having somewhere to rest your lovely head—rent free," he reminded, his voice tinged with impatience.

I crossed my arms over my chest again with a cluck of my tongue. "All right, let's forget your profession for the time being. Explain this to me. Wouldn't something like this house—a large, probably valuable piece of property—go into probate as a part of your estate? Or to a family member when they read your will? How can you just let me move into something that technically isn't even yours anymore? Or is that a super secret, too?"

I wasn't entirely dumb to human legal practices, if that's what Win was hoping. Possessions such as a house went into probate until your will was read and an inheritor named.

"I've got that all covered," was all he said.

I ran a hand over my damp, frizzing hair in aggravation. "Is an explanation out of the question? Because as an FYI, it's not *you* they'll be hauling out of here for squatting. It's me, and I'm no good in jail. I can't seem to make soap on a rope work for me."

"I doctored my will."

Suspicion instantly reared its ugly head. I lifted one eyebrow to convey as much. "How can you doctor something without a physical form here on this plane?"

"I bribed Madam Zoltar, the medium. She doctored. I instructed her on the doctoring."

"Medium?" I balked out loud and dismissed him with a wave of my hand. I hadn't said a word before, but now I couldn't contain myself. "You do know almost every human who claims to be a real medium is eyeball-deep in baloney, don't you? They steal your money and the only spirit they have contact with is the spiriting away of said money from your bank account."

"Have you gone mad? Are you telling me Madame Zoltar isn't a real medium? That she bamboozled me? The horror!" Win squealed.

I fought the impulse to grin. "Even as well loved as she seems to be by the community, that's *exactly* what I'm telling you. You've been had."

Now his grating sigh whispered across the room. "Of course I knew she was a fake. I was a spy, for Pete's sake, Stevie."

"Right. An international man of intrigue."

His silence made me decide to play out this game with him. I didn't know where it was leading, but he seemed like the kind of voice who liked a good cat and mouse. What spy didn't like a good cat and mouse?

"Okay, first, why did you choose Madam Zoltar to communicate with?"

"You'll find this odd, but it was her staunch belief in the afterlife. Even though she couldn't really communicate with the dead, she *wanted* to with everything in her. She still believed it was possible, whether she had or not. That touched me."

Fair enough. He'd clearly known what he was getting into with Madam Zoltar.

"So how did you get Madam Zoltar to doctor your will?"

"I made promises, Stevie. Dirty, dirty promises. Some of which left me feeling cheap and used."

"I can't believe I'm even asking, but I'm just going to cannonball into the deep end. What did you promise her? Spill." I tapped my toe and waited.

I was pretty sure I felt his eyes roll back in his head in aggravation before he said, "Oh, okay. I said I'd attend two séances and some medium convention called The Crystal Ball Is Your Oyster Con. Not a big deal in the scheme of things. And all I had to do was show up and do spooky stuff, like make the table levitate, maybe flicker the lights on and off. You know; typical séance fare."

"And in return she did what to your will?"

"Changed the name of the sole beneficiary of my worldly possessions at my lawyer's office from my greedy cousin Sal to someone else…"

"Wouldn't your lawyer know who the original beneficiary really was?"

"I'm counting on the fact that he comes from the Mesozoic era and is incredibly forgetful. It was frightfully easy. Madam Zoltar printed up a new, fake document under my instruction, and voila. Instant revision."

"So you had her break the law for you. A nice little old lady like that?"

"I would never have allowed her to be caught, and I broke the law to save this side of the pond from Cousin Sal. You'll thank me, should you ever meet."

It was my turn to sigh, tiring rapidly of the spy game. I plunked down on the bottom step of the huge staircase, mindless of the debris. "So you had her change it to who? What does that mean?"

"It means I left my house and all my worldly possessions to *you*."

Chapter 6

All the blood drained from my face. My mouth opened, but it didn't want to cooperate with words. Not even smallish ones. It just hung there, all unhinged.

"I can see by your jaw scraping the floor I've surprised you."

"Only confetti and a clown car would match my level of surprise."

Had he been kidding when he'd said he'd left the house to me? I looked out the big bay window in the parlor overlooking the Sound at the choppy gray waters and blinked.

"And I guess you want to know why I'd leave my most treasured possession to you, and not a family member—or the DIY Channel."

"I can't make a decision. I mean, there are a whole list of pros and cons I need to make before I decide if I want to know why."

"I left it to you because you need this house, and it needs you. And the afterlife says you need help, and, above all, you can be trusted."

I scratched my head. "Is this your big afterlife pay-it-forward? Am I the charity case of the millennium to make up for all the charity cases you ignored in your former life? What are they feeding you in the afterlife to make such a big decision?"

Win scoffed at me. "I'm insulted you think I ignored charity while I was here on Earth. That cuts deep."

"Do spies donate to charity?"

"You'd be surprised what we spies do for a good cause. Haven't you ever heard of Spies For Tots? Never mind. Scratch that. No one's supposed to know we exist."

I fought a chuckle. "So why would you leave all this to me? You don't even know me."

"Honesty?"

"Should there ever be anything else between an ex-witch and the specter who's attached himself to her like a boil on her butt?"

"The truth is, I can't stand Sal. He's a bag of utter dicks. He'll turn this place into some ugly eyesore full of sterile chrome, white walls, and high-tech gadgets. Also, he's awful. The kind of awful that kicks puppies and pulls walkers right out from under the elderly. A place like this needs attention to detail, Stevie; it needs to be filled with things from days gone by. It needs love. I didn't have time to change my will before my untimely demise, but when I found this place just before I died, I'd already decided to do just that. I just ran out of time. But that's all handled now."

"It needs a whole lot more than love. It needs a backhoe."

"Bite your tongue."

I let my arms rest on my knees and looked at the sprawling home, most of which I hadn't even seen yet. It could really be something, given serious attention. It could be a dream come true. My mind raced with the possibilities, the potential, but my life was a wreck. I didn't have time to babysit contractors and subcontractors. I needed to find a job and some self-worth.

"Listen, it was really weird…nice, but weird of you to leave me your dilapidated fixer-upper, but in the interest of giving this house some love, love costs money. In this case, it's going to cost a lot of money. I don't have enough money for my lunch. I certainly don't have enough to not only get a place like this up and running, but keep it running. So thanks, but you'd better start making dirty-dirty promises to another psychic to fix your will again. Oh, and while you're hanging around the afterlife, please tell them thank you for the sterling references."

I would smile at the trust and friendships I'd built over the years with many a spirit, but the loss was still so fresh, it felt wrong to feel anything but sorrow because it was just a memory and no longer my reality.

Still, Win wasn't giving up. "I have money."

Grabbing my purse, I began to make my way toward the front door, fully intending to take myself back to the hotel and come up with a plan B. Because this was on par with ludicrous. Who signed over all their money and possessions on the word of dead people to someone they didn't even know?

"So you said. But I can't access money from a man who essentially claims he doesn't exist anywhere but in his head."

"I didn't say I didn't exist. I said London would tell you they'd never heard of me. It doesn't mean I can't prove to you I have a bank account, Stevie, or that I didn't see to it that all my money becomes yours."

I reached for the rusty doorknob, only to watch it turn and seize up. Ah. I knew this sort of ghost. The kind who liked to play rough and dazzle me with his otherworldly powers.

I narrowed my eyes at the room. "You know, Winterbutt, under normal circumstances, I'd break out my wand and zap you right into plane eleven for even considering holding me hostage in this heap of a dump."

"Scary, Stevie. What's plane eleven?"

I smiled smugly. "The plane where anyone who's willfully taken a life spends their eternity. Serial killers, mass murderers. You know; the typical types."

"Then it's a good thing for me petulant ex-witch's wand is out of service."

"I'm not petulant. I'm skeptical. I've only just met you and so far I've found a dead body, been questioned in a possible murder investigation, slandered at my favorite taco truck, told I'm going to inherit a house straight out of *American Horror Story* and a buttload of money, and now you've threatened me. Forgive my hesitance to jump into your pool with both feet."

"I did not threaten you. I was just trying to keep you from making an unwise decision and at the same time, flexing my newbie ghost muscles, if you will."

I let go of the doorknob. "An unwise decision?"

"Stevie?"

"Winterbutt?"

"The time, please?"

My sigh of impatience rang in the wide entryway as I reached into my purse and pulled out my phone without disturbing Belfry. "It's five-fifteen. Do you have a hot afterlife date?"

"Check your bank account, please. The one at Paris Spells Savings and Loan, and tell me the balance."

I flicked my finger over the app to access my pathetic savings account, preparing to see the last of my miniscule thousand dollars depleting rapidly. I fully intended to hold the phone up to his faceless voice and prove to him he was crazy as a bedbug.

Oh. Hold that thought. How in the world…?

I knew I was openly gaping, but I couldn't help it.

"Do tell, what does your bank balance say, Stevie?" Win asked, a playful hint to his tone.

"Uh…a lot. It says…a lot of those lunches you mentioned," I muttered, unable to believe my eyes. "How did you…?

"I told you, Madam Zoltar and I had a deal of sorts. I talked to the dead for her; she helped me change my will."

But then a very nefarious thought hit me in the gut.

My hand went directly to my hip in righteous indignation. "How do I know it's not drug money, or laundered money, or just plain old dirty money?"

"Because I have immaculate tax records that are a testament otherwise."

"How do I know they're not forged or fakes? What if you made Madam Zoltar do something illegal and she didn't think to question you because she was so blown away by finally contacting the dead and your spiffy British accent?"

"Stevie…"

I sucked in my cheeks. "Am I trying your patience?"

"I didn't think anyone could match my irritation after the last jewel thief I apprehended in Monte Carlo, but you're this close."

"Ooo, did you have to crawl under deadly laser beams that could cut you in half if you moved a millimeter the wrong way to catch him?" I mocked.

"Stevie!" His voice reverberated through the house, bouncing off the fifteen-foot ceilings.

"Fine. Carry on."

"Please, if you'd indulge me, check your voice mail."

"I'm afraid."

"I promise not to think less of you for behaving so cowardly. Please check."

I clicked the app for my voice mail, noted there was a message, and put it on speaker. There was a crackle on the line and then, "Miss Cartwright? This is Davis Monroe, Esquire. I'd been instructed to contact you upon the confirmation of the death of one Crispin Alistair Winterbottom. Please return my call promptly, as we need to discuss your inheritance."

Forget my alleged inheritance—Winterbottom's first name was Crispin?

I began to laugh, my head falling back on my shoulders while I tried to catch my breath. "Crispin Alistair?" I sputtered.

Win cleared his throat. "Ahem. Pardon me, but it's a prestigious birthright and well respected where I come from. Certainly nothing a heathen like you would understand."

I snorted again, but I also realized I now had a name. A full name to research. *Google, be my guide.*

"Before you warm up your fingers to Google me, do note, you'll find nothing about my profession as a spy online. Crispin Alistair Winterbottom was a mild-tempered grade-school teacher, at least according to Google."

"Riiight. Got it. When you look me up? Don't believe LinkedIn and my former job as a 9-1-1 dispatcher. I'm really a prima ballerina with the Bolshoi Ballet."

"For your information, I wouldn't believe that even if I saw you in a tutu and tights, not after your blatant Peggy Fleming in Madam Zoltar's store."

"That's because you're a super spy with an antenna for lies, right?" Then I began to laugh again, bending forward at the waist to try to catch my breath.

"Can we please set aside the fact that you're calling me a liar and focus on the tasks at hand? I did just make you rich, did I not?"

I clicked on the app again and typed in my password. Yep. The money was all still there. But it didn't mean it was staying there or that it wasn't dirty.

"You did. You also gave me a house that's about to fall down around my ears. You're a total peach."

"This house can be restored to its former beauty and I know just the person. But we have other things to do right now. Right now, we have to help Madam Zoltar and find her killer."

My shoulders sagged as I hauled my purse to the crook of my arm. I was tired. It had been a long, grueling day. I wanted to go back to my cheap hotel room with the paper-thin blankets, take a shower and sleep for a year.

"Can we do that tomorrow?"

"And that brings me to this…"

"What's 'this'?"

"The deal."

I nodded my head knowingly. "You mean the strings, right? Because no one gives someone a boatload of money and a house on the bluff, even if it's falling to pieces, without strings. No one. What's the deal?"

"I propose this. You can have it all, *all* of it. My house, my money, my toothbrush, which is the only personal possession I own, aside from some very expensive suits, but only if you agree to work with me to help find who killed Madam Zoltar—"

"But—"

"I'm not done yet. You must also agree to renovate this house for me under my instruction, and you have to remain here until its completion."

I lifted my shoulders. "Is that all? So basically, give up my entire life to live in a drafty, dirty wreck and figure out who killed Madam Zoltar, all while everyone in town calls me a murderer?"

"You have no life, Stevie."

"That's mean."

"It's true."

My finger shot up in the air. "First of all, we don't even know she was killed. Maybe it was just a heart attack or a stroke or any number of things. Second, why the fudge don't you just ask Madam Z what happened yourself? You *are* in the afterlife with her, aren't you? She should have arrived by now. What kind of spy are you?"

"Now, Stevie," he said with that superior tone of his. "You know full well when a soul passes over after they've left your plane in a traumatic incident, they're confused and disoriented. Madam Zoltar is a wreck of emotions. She's gobsmacked, and no one can get through to her or understand all her rambling. She's been drifting around from plane to plane since this afternoon. But because she's so confused, that means only one thing. You know it and I know it. She was *murdered*."

"Why do you care so much about this woman, Win? What aren't you telling me?"

His reply was stiff and very British. "I've told you everything you need to know about my relationship with Madam Zoltar."

"So why does finding her murderer mean so much to you? You hardly knew her."

"Because justice should be served in healthy portions. And I liked her. I liked her a great deal. She reminded me of my grandmother. Not to mention, she helped keep this house and all my extraordinarily hard-earned money from my cousin Sal."

Something about the way he spoke, the warmth in his voice, made me cave just a little. Clearly, he'd grown fond of Madam Zoltar. But I also wondered how long he'd known her before she was killed. My impression was it had been a short relationship, yet his tone almost suggested otherwise.

Which begged the question… "Why did you put Sal's name on the will if you didn't want him to have the house?"

"Because when my lawyer called me to arrange the will, he phoned when I was at the height of a very delicate interrogation. I was pressed to name someone and then I forgot all about it. Sal is my only living relative. He was the first person to come to mind when the word 'familial' came into play."

"What do you suppose Sal will have to say about this startling turn of events?"

"He never knew he was named to begin with, so he won't say a thing."

"You don't have any friends? A BFF?"

"Spies don't have BFFs." His response was curt and screamed this area of his life was none of my business.

Tucking my chin in my hand, I parsed the deal out in words. "So all I have to do is stay here until the house is done, which could take a hundred years and a hundred backhoes, help you figure out who killed Madam Zoltar, and I can keep the money and the house?"

"And you must agree to renovating *my* way."

Really, what did I have to lose? If everything checked out, if the money was clean, it was just a house. It wouldn't eat up even a quarter of the money he'd dumped into my account, and I'd still be in the black. If nothing else, it meant Belfry and I would eventually have somewhere warm and dry to hang our hats.

"And you're sure there's no illegal attachment to this money or this house? Some drug lord from Constantinople won't come knocking on the door wanting his cash?"

"The chances of a drug lord from Constantinople are slim to none. Now, Columbia?" he rumbled. "That's a more distinct possibility."

"Winterbottom!"

"Joking. No drug lords or otherwise."

I took a deep breath and looked around at this heaping mess of debris and crumbling walls, rotted wood and graffiti from squatters, and as the light began to rapidly fade, I made a decision.

My first big, possibly life-changing decision as a human. As much as I longed to go back to my friends in Paris, as much as I missed being a witch, I was no longer welcome in the coven. So it was move on or give up.

I decided to move on.

"Okay. It's a deal. I'd shake on it but, well, you know—ghost and all."

"I'm thrilled right now. I wish you could see my face."

I wished I could see his face, too. It would be nice to have a face to attach to the whiskey-rough but smooth-as-melted-chocolate voice.

"Are you smiling?"

"I don't smile, I smirk."

"As all good spies do. So what do we do next?" I asked, reaching for the rusty doorknob.

"We plan a strategy, Stevie. A strategy to smoke out a killer."

"Can we do that after I have some dinner?"

"We can begin tomorrow. Bright and early."

I twisted the doorknob and was relieved to feel it turn beneath my fingers. "Oh, one more thing."

I felt the cool warmth of his aura surround me. I use the words cool and warm because he had the feel of a ghost in that spin-tingling sense, but his aura was warm. "What's that?"

"About that Aston Martin you mentioned…"

"Not even if your life was hanging in the balance."

I giggled as I stepped out onto the porch, using my phone as a flashlight to find my way down the stairs.

Something clicked inside me at that moment. Something felt innately right, and that was when I decided I felt more like myself than I had in over a month.

Just like the old Stevie, but without a wand and a curse-you-and-your-damnable-soul-to-the-fiery-depths-of-Hades spell.

Chapter 7

"Good morning, Mr. Sherwood!" I called as I entered the near-empty Strange Brew, the coffee shop next door to Madam Zoltar's.

The shop was filled with pastel-colored wrought iron tables, cheerful bud vases with pink carnations, and a glass counter with fat muffins in every flavor imaginable. I liked the vibe in here.

It was easy on the eye, and the smooth coffeehouse jazz playing over the sound system soothed my nerves for what I was about to do. Which was behave as though Chester Sherwood had never accused me of murdering "his" Tina. Keep your enemies close and all.

"How about you not be so nice to the guy who accused you of hurting 'his Tina'," Belfry chirped from inside my purse, still cross he'd missed my deal-making with Winterbottom.

When he'd heard about our newfound riches, he'd been thrilled. Until he heard I didn't fight for the Aston Martin. Then he'd pouted for two hours after the most sumptuous breakfast I'd had in years—courtesy of my fat bank account. After taking a cab into Seattle and finding a place to dine where no one would label me a murderer, I'd treated Belfry and myself to the first decent meal we'd had in weeks.

There'd be plenty of lunches I'd have to eat while skulking in some cold alleyway, considering the hate everyone in town was expressing about my alleged involvement with Madam Zoltar's death. I figured it was only fair we begin the day pampered.

"Chester's a fine man, Belfry. He was simply reacting to his grief. It's natural."

"This from the man who waterboards criminals for a living? What do you know about grief, Winterbutt?" Belfry squeaked in outrage.

I didn't understand this sudden animosity toward Win. Belfry had been all sorts of determined to involve me with him and now he was behaving as though he'd never swooned over his accent just a mere twenty-four hours ago.

But Win just chuckled, rich and deep. "I might not know grieving, but I can assure you, Cheeky One, I know how to dole out some grief."

Belfry growled from the interior of my purse, fluffing his wings for hand-to-wing combat. "Was that a threat, Spy Guy?"

"Belfry!" I held my purse up to my face, pretending I was rooting around for my debit card. "Knock it off. You started this, and now we're in—both feet. Adjust, buddy, and stop being so rude. We have a place to live and money in our pockets thanks to Win. Remember the whole attitude-is-gratitude talk over breakfast while you gobbled down lush mangos and kiwi?"

"We have a dump, that's what we have. A cold, ugly, ramshackle dump from the seventh circle of hell."

Fair enough. We did have a dump, but I'd already been in touch with the "someone" Win had in mind for the renovations, and he was assessing things as I stood here. I'd also been in touch with Davis Monroe, Esquire, and I did indeed have not just a great deal of money, but the deed to a house Crispin Alistair Winterbottom had bought just two months prior to his mysterious death—*with cash.*

When I'd inquired about Win's passing, the only information Davis Monroe was able to provide was the death certificate he'd received from London.

Upon receipt of a death certificate, he'd been instructed by Win to consider him expired and the reading of his will should commence exactly a month from the day of his passing, which was two days ago as per Davis Monroe.

Win had explained how he'd left the timeframe for announcing his death at a month as a safeguard. It was in case he wasn't really dead. According to him, sometimes spies went deep undercover, and even their superiors had to pretend they were dead.

Davis Monroe was only to accept a death certificate from a source Win had named in his will—someone he trusted beyond reproach, and someone who could, without a shadow of a doubt, confirm he was gone.

I'd mentally put the date of his expiration in my box of things to explore once I could find a moment alone with Google sans Win in my ear.

I panicked for a moment when Mr. Monroe mentioned how odd it was that he could have sworn there'd been an entirely different name listed as Crispin Winterbottom's sole beneficiary, but he chalked it up to the hectic phone call with a lot of background noise (which, according to Win, was in the middle of an interrogation) and his age. Which was nearing eighty, but he was still fit as a fiddle, he'd joked.

So I learned Win hadn't been dead for long. That he'd acclimated so quickly to the afterlife said something about his fortitude. Sometimes it took weeks to find your footing as a ghost if you chose to wait on crossing over.

But not Spy Guy. He had it down. What he'd said about the confusion and disorientation a soul experiences if their death was traumatic was also true. So did that mean he didn't die a traumatic spyworthy death? Or was he just tough as nails?

That he'd had so many rigid rules and instructions in his will in preparation for his death spoke volumes about who he was when he was alive.

Orderly (well, except for naming Sal as his sole beneficiary, but who could blame a guy when he was in the middle of a delicate grilling?), concise, and no-nonsense.

But I still didn't know why the house meant so much to him or if he really had been a spy.

However, I decided to let it go for the time being in favor of catching a killer. There was no immediacy to finding a job now. Though find one I would, when this was through. Money was lovely. It meant security, but it didn't mean I wanted to sit on my butt without purpose.

So I set my sights on keeping my promise to Win by doing what I once did best. Solving a puzzle. I didn't love that I'd be solving them minus my spells and wand, but this felt good—to be back at a place in my life where I wasn't in limbo.

I closed my purse and waved to Chester Sherwood as I approached. He sat at a corner table with a single pink carnation in a vase, his plaid shirt crisp, his eyes behind his glasses sharp.

He was reading the local paper. My stomach dashed to my feet, stopping me in my tracks when I read the headline: *Beloved Local Medium Allegedly Murdered—Suspect Questioned.*

So now I was a *confirmed* suspect. As far as I knew, I was the only one questioned. Darn, and this day had started out so shiny and new.

"Don't let it get in your head, Stevie. Do what you came to do," Win coached.

I plastered a smile on my face for Chester's benefit. "Hi, Mr. Sherwood, remember me from yesterday?" *Duh, stupid. How could he forget? He accused you of murder.*

He looked over the top of his morning paper, his round glasses sitting at the end of his nose. "The murderer."

If there was one thing that never changed about Ebenezer Falls, word got around just as quickly as ever. It wouldn't be long before everyone else was calling me a murderer, too.

I pulled out the chair opposite him and asked with a smile, "May I?"

"Don't ask, Stevie. Just sit. Own this interrogation," Win demanded in brisk words.

I held up a finger and said, "Just one moment, please, Mr. Sherwood," before I turned my back to him and whispered from the side of my mouth. "What did I tell you about interfering? We made rules this morning, Win. I was very clear about how we'd do this—"

"Among other things," Win drawled. "What was rule number fifty-six again? Something about announcing my entrance to any room with the mating call of the North American—"

"He's not a suspect in a terrorist attack or a valuable art heist, Win! He's an elderly gentleman who may have seen something yesterday he doesn't think is important but could help Madam Zoltar, and more importantly, us. Now put away the bamboo shoots to jam under his nails and *back off!*"

I turned back around and cleared my throat, putting a finger to my ear and pointing at the Bluetooth earpiece I planned to use as a beard whenever Win decided I needed his spy-erly advice. "Sorry. An unexpected call from one of those naggy telemarketers. Anyway, may I sit with you? Please?"

Mr. Sherwood dropped his paper to his lap and glared at me. "Why would I wanna sit with you? And just so's you know, I don't care how pretty you are. You ain't winnin' me over with those big blue eyes. You're still a murderer. The paper says so."

I pouted, deciding to use my big blue eyes to my advantage even though they weren't so much blue as a boring gray.

"Aw, c'mon, Mr. Sherwood. I'd never hurt a fly. I know what you think, and what everyone's saying, but I swear on my honor, I just went in to take a look around and got clumsy. I grew up here and so much has changed. Madam Zoltar's used to be a sewing shop when I was a kid. So I was curious to see the changes and maybe meet Madam Zoltar."

Now he was interested. I saw it in his expression. "Who's your kin?"

But this was where things could get sticky for me. My mother didn't exactly have a stellar reputation. She'd been quite the cougar back in the day—or gold digger, depending on which of her victims you asked.

Still, I couldn't lie about who she was. Maybe he'd even feel sorry for me.

"Dita Cartwright was my mother."

He bobbed his balding head, his lips still in a thin line of disapproval. "Yep. Lived over in the fancy cul-de-sac, didn't ya? That explains your good looks."

"You knew my mother?" I asked before I thought better. Opening up the subject of my mother was always tricky business. You never knew who you'd run into when it came to a stranger's experience with the infamous Dita. Sometimes they were friends, but more likely they were angry, bitter foes.

"Yep," he offered before returning to his paper.

This was going exactly as I'd planned. Or not. Ugh.

The man behind the counter, whose back had been turned, saved me having to offer up excuses about Dita when he approached the table, a pad in his hand.

When I looked up, I almost fell out of my chair.

Why hadn't I remembered Forrest Sherwood when Win told me Chester's last name? Two years older than me, he was the hottest thing Ebenezer Falls High School had to offer back in the day.

I jumped up and stuck out my hand. "Forrest? I had no idea you were in town! It's Stevie. Stevie Cartwright! I was two years behind you, but we went to school together, remember?"

Forrest smiled slow and easy, making deep grooves appear on either side of his mouth. He took my hand and nodded. "I didn't at first, but I knew your name was familiar when Grandpa told me about what happened yesterday. Stevie's an unusual name for a woman. Black lipstick, long trench coat, right?"

I waved my hand in the air at him and giggled. "All day, every day. That was me and my signature brand of Goth."

"Could you be any more schoolgirl-crush obvious?" Win blustered in my ear.

I stuck my middle finger up behind my head in the direction of Win's voice as I tucked my hair back into place and sat in my chair.

"You've *really* changed," he said with his boy-next-door grin, eyeing my thrift store pink and gray Hermes scarf I'd so carefully wrapped around my neck and draped down my chest to cover the hole in my second-hand silk shirt.

The shirt was tucked into my third favorite pair of jeans to also hide the wasabi stain on the hem, and I'd paired it all with work boots because I'd sold most of my thrift-store shoes before I left Paris.

So while I'm sure I looked different, I was still the girl who dripped ketchup down the front of her when she was eating a hot dog.

But I grinned back at Forrest, brushing my hair from my eyes and setting my sunglasses on top of my head. "I have indeed. For the better, I hope."

"So your hair really wasn't that black with the purple glow?"

"Nope. I've always been a boring medium brown. My quest to be different from everyone else wasn't always a success."

Forrest laughed, deep and rumbly. "Well, you look terrific."

Win's sigh went long and raspy-loud straight through my eardrums. "God save the Queen. Let's get on with this. This isn't bloody eHarmony. This is an interrogation."

"So you work here?" I asked Forrest, noting his hair was still as sunshiney blond and his eyes were still just as aquamarine as they'd been back when we were in school.

Chester dropped his newspaper altogether and glared at me. "He owns the place."

Forrest put his hand on his grandfather's shoulder and gave it a light squeeze before snapping one of his red suspenders. "Gramps? Ease up, huh? You don't really believe Stevie hurt Madam Zoltar, do you? Be nice to the customers. Especially ones as pretty as Stevie—and stop perpetuating the rumor."

Chester blustered. "Don't you go givin' me your PC nonsense about shaming and whatever else it is you extra-sensitive kids have come up with to get all up in arms about!"

I preened extra hard for Win's benefit before I asked, "Speaking of Madam Zoltar, do you mind if I ask you a couple of questions about her, Mr. Sherwood?"

"Finally," Win groused.

Mr. Sherwood grumbled, adjusting his suspenders and shrugging Forrest off. "What do you wanna know? And remember, I'm immune to those big gray-blue eyes a yours."

I winked playfully. "Right. I dub thee immune. So, before you heard me knocking around next door like an elephant doing the fandango, did you see anything else, hear anything else?"

"Nope. I'm hard a hearin'. Surprised the nonsense right outta me when I heard the ruckus. I was sittin' right over there at that corner table havin' a latte-schmatte-mocha-choca-ya-ya or whatever the kid here calls 'em. 'Bout knocked me out of my chair. So you know it was daggone loud."

I looked to my left at the row of sherbet-colored wrought iron tables and noted the wall of Strange Brew faced the very wall where I'd demolished the metal rack with all the candles.

"And what time did you get here to your grandson's shop, Mr. Sherwood?"

"What are you, a Charlie's Angel? I don't even know why you're askin', but I got here at six-thirty. Same time I do every day."

"You know," Forrest interrupted, pulling up a chair to sit between us, his long legs knocking into mine. "Now that you mention it, I do remember hearing a yelp at around eight-thirty or so. But I just figured it was one of the kids walking to the bus stop for school. They're always pretty noisy and full of it, so I didn't think anything about it. You don't think it was Mrs. Martoni, do you? I'd feel awful if she needed help and I..."

Forrest looked stricken by the idea he might have missed saving her. But that niggle from last night hadn't gone away. I don't think anyone could have helped her.

Folding my hands in front of me, I looked for a sign with the hours of Strange Brew, but didn't see one. "What time does the coffee shop open, Forrest?"

"I open at six sharp every day for the commuters and early birds. There are lots of 'em that take the sunrise yoga class three times a week at Joy Carmichael's studio just three doors down."

I tapped my finger on my chin. "Isn't that a rather strange hour for Madam Zoltar to open up shop? I thought most psychics kept nighttime hours?" When it was easier to pull off fake séances and flickering lights.

Chester tapped his newspaper with a thick forefinger, his face still quite cross. "Tina lived in the back of the shop. She always opened early for any commuters who might want a tarot card reading."

Now I was going to tread into sensitive waters. Chester's tone and staunch defense of Madam Zoltar yesterday made me wonder if he'd had romantic notions about her. "You liked Madam Zoltar a great deal. It's obvious. Were the two of you close friends?"

Forrest barked a laugh as Chester's round cheeks went rosy. "Mrs. Martoni—as I called her, anyway—was a little sweet on Gramps, I think. But Gramps only has eyes for Gram. I told him he had to stop referring to her as 'his', but it's just his way of declaring how much he cares about her."

So an unrequited love on Madam Z's part, maybe? Hmmm. "That's so sweet, Chester. Your wife's lucky to have someone as upstanding as you."

Chester finally looked at me, but his eyes were no longer hard like ice chips, they were melancholy and soft. "My Violet's gone now. Just like Tina. Like to think she met her at the Pearly Gates and welcomed her inside."

I swallowed hard and without thought, reached out and gripped his hand. "I'm sorry, Mr. Sherwood."

He squeezed my hand back before he pushed his chair out, obviously done with my questions and done with me. "Anything else you wanna harass me about, *Kojack*?"

I refused to let him thwart my efforts to make friends. Someday, sooner than Chester Sherwood thought, we'd share a cup of coffee—maybe even a muffin—and he'd like it, or I'd die trying.

"Just one more thing, please?" I smiled sweetly. I'd seen my mother do it a thousand times if I'd seen her do it once, and it almost always worked.

Chester frowned as though he were visibly fighting the forces of my evil. "What?"

Okay, I'd have to work on my flirty smiles. "Did you see anyone else go into Madam Zoltar's store at all that morning?"

"I already told ya, I was sittin' over there by the wall that faces her store. Can't see nothin' but the street from that vantage point, Sherlock Holmes. That's where I sat until I heard those elephant feet a yours, tearin' up the joint. It's where I sit every day. Are we done now, Blue Eyes? Because *The Price Is Right's* comin' on and I got a date with some Victoria's Secret models for lunch."

I laughed out loud. "You've been very indulgent with this accused murderer, but I think I'm good now. Thanks much, Mr. Sherwood. I hope to see you again really soon."

He flapped his hand at me, but I'd swear on my wand, he had to fight a reluctant smile as he trotted off behind the counter and toward the kitchen.

Forrest leaned into me just enough to remind me he was still there. "Sorry about Gramps. He can be a real ornery coot, but he's a good guy and I can tell he's warming to you."

"Oh, I'll win him over eventually. Speaking of winning someone over, you said you thought Mrs. Martoni was sweet on him?"

"He and Mrs. Martoni talked all the time, but Gramps never saw it. Everyone else did, but not him. He was interested in only one thing."

I let my hand rest in my chin and asked, "What was that?"

"I really think he believed Mrs. Martoni, aka Madam Zoltar, could get in touch with my grandmother on the other side."

I fought a healthy dose of skepticism again, forcing my eyes not to roll and give away my stance on mediums. Poor Chester.

"Did she try?"

Forrest bobbed his head. "She did, and it brought a comfort to him I can't explain, but I have to admit I was grateful to her. He never told me what actually happened when she tried to contact Gram, but he came back a different man. Still cranky as all get out, but more at peace, I guess would be the word. I can't really explain it. Either way, they were friends. She came in all the time for coffee and they'd shoot the breeze. He'd bring her a muffin from time to time."

My heart ached for Chester Sherwood and his lost love. Sometimes grief made you reach out in the oddest of ways, but it sounded as though his friendship with Madam Z comforted him.

"If you don't mind me asking, how long has your grandmother been gone?"

Forrest's smile was fond, but far away. "Two years now. Miss her a lot."

"Then I'm glad your grandfather had Madam Zoltar for a friend."

Forrest shook off his reverie and turned to me as he prepared to rise, his eyes sparkling even in the gloom of the day. "So how long are you in town, Stevie?"

"Oh, I'm back for good." That was the first time I'd acknowledged Paris was never going to be my home again. Which had to be a healthy sign I'd accepted my fate and was moving on—at least for now.

"That's good to know. Would you grab dinner with me sometime?"

Win groaned in my ear, but I blushed from head to toe. "I'd love to. But I have to run for now. It was great seeing you, Forrest."

Pushing his chair out, he tilted his well-groomed head toward the counter. "Cup of coffee for the road? My treat."

My hand went to the knot in my scarf. "I'd love one."

"*I'd love one*," Win repeated, mimicking me. I pictured him rolling his head on his neck and flipping his pretend hair. "Let's get on with this for bloody sake, Stevie."

But I flapped him away as I sauntered to the counter on a cloud. Forrest Sherwood had asked me out. *Take that, Sandy McNally.*

Just as I was hovering on my cloud and bemusing how shocked Sandy would be to find Forrest had asked out the town rebel in black instead of the prettiest high school cheerleader, the door to the coffee shop bounced open, a gust of sharp wind blowing in through the door.

Sandwich filled the store with his sheer bulk. His cheeks were their usual beet red, his shortly cropped hair springing from his scalp. "There you are, Stevie! Been all over town lookin' for you. I thought you were stayin' out at the hotel by the cliffs?"

Accepting my coffee from Forrest with a smile, I turned to say, "I was, but my plans changed."

"Don't you check your phone?"

"What's going on, Sandwi—" I paused and looked around the shop, just beginning to fill with the lunch crowd. I remembered his words from yesterday and caught myself. "Um, I mean, Lyn. What's up?"

He huffed his way toward me, leaving wet size-twelve footprints on the shiny wood flooring. "You're gonna have to come with me."

"Now what did I do?"

He leaned in, keeping his voice low, his eyes rounded with pleading. "Don't make a scene, Stevie, *please*. Just come with me."

I moved my finger like a metronome. "Aw, heck no. No can do, old friend. The last time I went with you, I spent an hour swearing on my favorite knock-off Coach bag that I didn't know anything about what happened to Madam Zoltar. And look where it's gotten me? Right back here with you in my face. My answers haven't changed since yesterday. There's absolutely nothing else I can tell you other than I found Madam Zoltar exactly the way you did, and I had nothing to do with how she died. In fact, how *did* she die, Sandwich? The local paper called it murder. Is that the verdict? Am I the 'suspect' the paper mentioned?"

At that point, my words began to bleed into each other, which only served to frustrate Sandwich. Beads of sweat broke out on his brow.

"The preliminary reports say she was strangled." Then he blanched. "I'm not supposed to tell you this! Stop talking so fast."

I gasped. "She was *strangled*? But what about the hole in her foot?" Instantly, I regretted my reaction, wanting nothing more than to stuff my fist in my big mouth as the lunch crowd turned to stare at me.

The charred skin on the ball of her foot screamed electrocution. But then I remembered the scarf around her neck. Maybe I'd missed any signs of strangulation because I'd been so hung up on a different cause of death.

However, why in seven hells was the ball of her foot burned? Did she step on something? I had to get into that store and at least take a look around.

And another thing, how good had Spy Guy been as a spy if he didn't have any theories yet?

I gripped Sandwich's arm, looking up at him. "Are you sure she was strangled? Are the papers right? Are they really now calling Madam Zoltar's death *murder?*"

He bounced from foot to foot with nervous energy, running his index finger along the collar of his stiff shirt. "Stop asking me questions, Stevie. You know I can't answer them."

Crossing my arms over my chest, coffee cup against my chin, I eyed him. "Then that makes us even, because I can't answer yours either."

"Aw, c'mon," he pleaded under his breath. "Don't make a big deal of this, just come to the station, talk to the lead detective and you're done."

"They've definitely involved detectives?" I hadn't been sure if who I saw yesterday was a genuine detective going into MZ's. But this meant an official investigation was underway, didn't it? Human laws and witch laws were so different, I wasn't sure.

Sandwich sort of pouted. "I can't tell you that. Please, just take a ride to the station with me."

"And if I refuse? Am I then under arrest, Officer Paddington?"

Now he looked uncomfortable. "Shoot no, Stevie. We just want to ask you more questions is all."

Win breezed into my ear then. "Might I remind you, Stevie Like-Nicks-the-Singer, you don't have to answer anything without a lawyer present unless they're arresting you. A lawyer you can well afford now."

I turned away from a confused Sandwich, putting my hand to the Bluetooth piece in my ear, and muttered, "Won't that cut into our house budget and that fancy claw-foot tub you were babbling about this morning?"

I wasn't used to having bags of money, let alone the amount now sitting in my bank account. It's why I bought all of my clothes in thrift stores and consignment shops. Because I loved designer duds, I just couldn't afford them.

"Hardly," Win drawled.

Then that settled that. I turned back to my former classmate and gave him the haughtiest look I had in my arsenal, condescending raised eyebrow and everything.

"Sandwich? You go right back to your captain and tell him Stevie Cartwright won't be questioned without her lawyer present, and if they want me to come in any other way, they'll have to arrest me!"

"Stevieee," Sandwich groaned. "They sent me because I know you—"

"And they thought they'd use that familiarity to abuse my good nature, didn't they?"

Sandwich scratched his head, his shoulders slumping. "I think so. Er, no. I don't know…"

I dropped my coffee cup on a nearby table and turned, putting my hands behind my back in a submissive gesture. "Well? Either you cuff me or I'm walking out that door, Sandwich." And for the benefit of the crowd of people staring at me as though I had two heads and three breasts, I said, "Because I am not, I repeat, I am *not* a murderer!"

As everyone's eyes widened, I stomped to the door, forgetting my coffee, forgetting everything except for my pride. I still had that.

Well, mostly.

When I stomped back and scooped up my coffee with shaky hands, I somehow managed to fumble the cup. My scarf now askew from my temper tantrum, I spilled the hot liquid all down the front of my silk shirt.

The shirt that suddenly became quite see-through.

Ugh.

Chapter 8

"The good news is, you had a bra on, Stevie. I've seen more skin on *SpongeBob SquarePants* than you were showing."

Belfry's attempt to make me feel better wasn't helping.

"If you only knew how much I wish I lived in a pineapple under the sea right now!" I whisper-yelled.

"I didn't see a thing. Pinky spy swear," Win chimed in with his support.

I stomped up the street, passing Tito my taco vendor, who had the audacity to turn his back on me the moment I came into view, but not before he gave me the evil eye.

Several people, tucked into their winter vests and knit hats, literally looked the other way as I stalked along the curb toward nowhere in particular.

But when one of the shop owners, sweeping the sidewalk along his store, looked at me with obvious suspicion, I think I officially lost it a little.

Enough was enough. I stopped right in the middle of the sidewalk, raised my fists to the gloomy sky, and bellowed at him and anyone else in my path, "*I am not a murderer!*"

"Stevie! Steady the hull, huh? It's like being on a roller coaster in here, for cripes' sake!"

I winced, cradling my purse to my chest and peering into the interior with remorse. Poor Belfry.

I sucked in a deep breath of cool air to ease the tightness in my chest. "Sorry, buddy. I kind of flipped my nut there."

"Tell me again why we decided to come back to Seattle? I almost think it would have been better to stay in Paris and take those batty witches and all their guff. At least you knew your enemy."

"Didn't they call me a murderer there, too?" I regretted saying as much the moment the words came out of my mouth, but there they were. All out in the open and so very ugly.

"Come again?" Win whispered in my ear, his presence there now quite cold.

Belfry poked his head out the top of my purse. "Aw, leave her alone, Winterbutt. She's had a rough month."

"Aw. Poor Boo. I died. Whaddya have to top that?"

I knew I'd eventually have to explain to Win why I no longer was a part of my coven, and where my powers had gone, but in some passive, pathetically misguided notion, I'd hoped someone in the afterlife would tell him for me. In this case, I was almost glad I couldn't see his face. He hadn't pressured me about it, but I wanted to be open about my ability to help.

"I said leave her alone, or I'm gonna fly up outta this musty den of lipstick and tampons and—"

"Belfry! Stop. It's okay. I do owe Win an explanation."

"Like the one he gave *you* about what happened to *him*?" Belfry yelped with disbelief.

"I've just given you everything I own, including a hefty sum of money. I'd think an explanation would be a courtesy you'd want to extend. But if you'd prefer, I can wait. No pressure here."

That was more than fair. He should know whom he was doing business with.

I stopped at the corner just past the coffee shop and darted across the street to the bus stop shelter, where at least I'd be dry while I laid my baggage on the carousel for Win to see.

Dropping down to the seat, I looked out at the dismal day, musing at how it mirrored my emotions. "Okay, so first of all, 'murderer' is a little dramatic. Only one person actually said that, and while most of my friends rushed to defend me, it didn't make hearing it any easier. I guess that particular accusation kind of stuck with me."

"So you're not a murderer then?" Win asked in his no-nonsense way.

"Didn't anyone in the afterlife tell you how I ended up losing my powers?"

The first week after I'd suffered the loss, Belfry had fended off more inquiries than the Spanish Inquisition. Most of them had come in like messages on an old ham radio, full of static and choppy, but the distress from my ethereal pals shone through. That time in my life still ached. I missed communicating with the spirits—I missed helping them.

Win cleared his throat. "I've heard many things, but nothing clear. Whatever happened, everyone here is rather apprehensive to say much, I'm guessing. I sense some fear in their tones when they refer to the incident."

"And still you trusted me with a frillion dollars and Mayhem Manor?"

"Is that the name you're suggesting we put on the sign along the drive?"

I folded my cold hands in my lap and shrugged my shoulders. "I wasn't suggesting anything, really. It just popped into my head, considering the condition of the place. But it has a ring to it. Like, it's sort of all encompassing, don't you think?"

"Um, no. No, I don't think. Stop avoiding the issue and tell me what's on your mind."

Oooo. Win was using his serious voice. Okay, house name tabled for now.

"So no one has told you how I lost my powers."

I didn't say it out loud, but I was sure it had to do with the severity of the accusation and whom the accusation had come from. Even in death, the son of a butt-scratcher wielded authority.

"Nothing clear. Though, I'm told the longer I'm here, the clearer things will become. Time served is an asset here, apparently."

That was true, too. The more time Win spent undecided about his eternal fate, the more the others in the same predicament would become sharper, more defined, and above all, more trusting.

"So what exactly did they tell you about me, Win? It had to have been enough to trust me with all your money."

"Truthfully? I would have given the money to the devil himself rather than hand it over to Sal. This wasn't all an altruistic act on my part, Stevie. I want to see my dream come to fruition. The word on this plane is, you're the one to trust. I thought, who better than a homeless woman down on her luck to help me live out my dream? You needed a place to stay, I had the place."

"Aw, you say the sweetest things. I'm all aglow with that special feeling only someone who's been haphazardly chosen at random to win the booby prize can feel."

Somehow, I'd figured there'd been much more thought to this decision he'd roped me into. Obviously, almost anyone would have done. I cracked my knuckles and stared out into the street, but Win was all business.

"But hold on. Now that I think back on it, I remember one woman, Marjorie Biddlesworth, I believe. Just before she walked into that annoying glare of a light, she said that you were railroaded. Does that have to do with what you're about to tell me?"

My memory of Margie was a fond one, making me smile. "Margie was an adorably cranky quilter who wanted to be sure Sissy-Sue Leeland didn't get any of her originally designed quilting patterns. She was adamant Sissy-Sue would steal them and call them her own."

"So what did Marjorie mean when she said you were railroaded?"

"Aside from my medium duties, I was a 9-1-1 dispatcher in my small town of Paris, Texas. One night I took a call from a very frightened little boy…" I bit the inside of my cheek to keep tears from forming in my eyes.

"And then?" Win asked with a much gentler tone.

"It was a domestic dispute, and when we take a call from the home of an authority figure in the coven, we're supposed to notify a superior immediately. Which I did, but I didn't do as I was told when handling the call."

My stomach began that infernal rumbling of turmoil and the wave of nausea not even a purging spell would rid me of.

Belfry rustled a wing, his indignant tone in full swing. "Those crackpots told her to tell the poor kid help was on the way and then hang up! To this day, I still can't believe they dismissed all the good Stevie did all those years just because she wouldn't leave a freaked-out seven-year-old in a state of hysteria without anyone to comfort him."

I nodded my head. "Belfry's right. They did tell me to hang up because the caller, a little boy named Peyton, was a council member's son. He was hysterical, sobbing almost so uncontrollably I couldn't figure out what he was saying, but it was clear he was petrified. I couldn't just leave him like that. Not even for a second. Help was well on its way, but he kept begging me to help him—to stay with him. Even when I told him someone would be there in seconds. I heard his mother screaming in the background and his father yelling…and Peyton was so terrified. He made me swear on my favorite candy I'd stay on the phone with him…"

There was absolutely no way I was letting go of a connection with a little boy who'd likely seen more in his seven years of life than I had in over thirty-two on this plane. So I did. I stayed right until the bitter end. And make no mistake, the end was indeed bitter.

"So you disobeyed a direct order and stayed on the phone with the little chap. Then what?"

My hands tightened into fists, the way they always did when I retold this story. "I did, and I damn well won't apologize for it. I hung up the official line, but I dialed him right back on my personal cell. He was so, so scared. At that point, I'd managed to calm him enough that he explained he just didn't want to be alone anymore when the 'bad' things happened. He said he usually hid in the closet when they fought, but this was the 'worstest' fight they'd ever had. He said his mommy always had bruises on her and broken bones from his daddy 'playing too rough.' It was all I could do not to snap my fingers and summon him from that despicable pig, but…"

"But council business is council business." Belfry chirped his mocking disdain.

Shaking off my reverie, I nodded. "Yes. That's the rule, but there was just no way I was hanging up. He never had anyone he could trust all his life, but in that moment of sheer terror, I vowed to be the first.

Anyway, to make a very long, gruesome story short, help arrived just a little too late."

I had my suspicions about why help arrived so late, but that was neither here nor there at this point.

"Please don't tell me the little fellow was harmed, Stevie. Just don't. I've been to hell and back. I've seen things that would curl your pretty toes. But children are sacred. They must always be protected at all costs." Win's voice was thick with emotion, surprising me.

I wondered about his vehemence on Peyton's behalf and what incident in his past had brought him to such strong words, but then, I felt the same way he did.

"No. Thank the goddesses, he wasn't harmed," I reassured.

I heard him release a breath in my ear, his presence once more warm. "So what happened next?"

"During the course of the call, Peyton's father had no idea he'd called 9-1-1 and—"

Now Win gasped. "His father caught him, didn't he, the slimy arse?" he growled low and feral.

Gulping, I nodded once more. "Yes. He caught him talking to me. Something he was strictly forbidden to do. Tell…he wasn't *ever* supposed to tell," I whispered with a shiver.

"But that jerkface, power-trippin' megalomaniac got his, didn't he, Stevie!" Belfry cried.

Closing my eyes to ward off the visions I'd created in my head about that night, I shivered. "Through an ironic turn of events, Peyton's father dragged him out of the closet and started down the steps with him. But in his rage, a rage so real and so terrifying I heard it clear through the phone, he tripped and fell down the steps and broke his neck."

We sat silently for a moment; me, reliving little Peyton Westfield's screams of horror, Win, clearly absorbing my words.

"*How*—how could this coven of yours have possibly blamed you for the death of a monster, Stevie? Is there no justice even in the paranormal world?" he bellowed into my ear, making me jump and wince.

I shrugged. It was the only way to express how utterly defeated and boggled by the event I still was. "It wasn't so much his death as it was the fact that Peyton's mother denied all of it. She denied her husband ever laid a hand on her. Even though I heard her screaming to stop. Despite the fact that I sat with Peyton for those terrifying three minutes while he begged me not to hang up and I heard every single threat that pig made."

"But wasn't there a phone record of what he'd done? How could one deny the physical proof of his brutality? Surely there were marks on her? Bruises?" Win spat.

"You forget, we're witches, Win. We can heal plenty of things with just a spell. It just takes a flick of the wrist. As to a record of the call? Yes, there's the first thirty or forty seconds of the official 9-1-1 call Peyton made to me. But the threats his father was making weren't clear. There was a lot of fuzzy yelling, and Peyton's mother claimed they were just having a heated discussion about football."

And that had been my downfall, the beginning of the end. Ann Westfield's staunch denial that her husband, the esteemed, Adam Westfield, council member extraordinaire, was anything but a good, kind husband who'd slipped and fallen down the stairs, and her insistence that little Peyton had just *misunderstood* the situation.

What hurt worse was the fact that Peyton's mother didn't address his trauma. She'd swept the whole mess right under the rug, as if the first seven years of his life had all been a figment of his imagination. She'd gaslighted Peyton to save her own dang hide—to avoid the retribution of the coven for not taking little Peyton far away from his father. For not protecting him. She was the very definition of battered-wife syndrome.

Yep. That happens in the witch world just as often as it does in the human.

"So the bloody bastard ended up dead. Good on him," Win growled. "But I still don't understand how that's enough cause for your witch powers to be taken away. Were they taken from you because you disobeyed an order from a superior?"

And here's the most ironic part yet of my return to the human world. "No. I knew I'd be punished for disobeying, but nothing so severe as what happened next."

"Because that's when *pow*!" Belfry yelped for effect.

"Pow?" Win asked.

Squeezing my temples with two fingers, I sighed. "Peyton's father wasn't just a council member—he was a very powerful warlock. One of the *most* powerful. And obviously he was angry about me comforting his abused son. So angry, he had another soul contact me once he'd arrived in the afterlife. This soul, no doubt held hostage by Peyton's father, was forced to fool me into believing he needed my help."

The wind whistled as Spy Guy digested. "You helped, I gather?"

I squirmed on the bus shelter's hard seat, locking my cold fingers together. "Of course I did. It's what I do."

"And the powerful warlock stole your powers."

"Slapped 'em right out of me straight from the afterlife."

Literally, he'd taken his hand, palm open, wound his arm up, and laid one on me. Adam Westfield hit me so hard, he'd stripped me bare of every last power I'd ever cultivated.

101

He left me naked. He took my home, my job, my life, in just the way he claimed I'd taken his. My throat tightened as I tugged on my scarf to stave off my helplessness. I would not cry. Not today.

"I'm sorry, Stevie. What an abominable way to lose something so integral to you."

I heard the remorse in Win's apology. I even felt the warmth of his aura surrounding me, and for some reason, it was important that he believed me.

"May I ask why you left your hometown and the people you love?"

Scraping a thumb under my eye to keep my tears at bay, I finished my story. "I was shunned. Told to pack my bags and leave because I was no longer like everyone else."

"Baba Yaga, The Imperial Empress of All Things Witch, booted her butt out without so much as a thank you for keeping that poor kid calm and alive. Little Peyton would be dead if not for Stevie. I told that stupid bunch of crusty old bones as much when I called council, but they wouldn't listen. Not that Peyton's testimony helped Stevie's cause any. His mother coached him to say nothing happened, and I'll swear that's what she did on my dying breath. None of the good Stevie did mattered. Not a dang shred of it. So essentially, they said it was her own fault the Wingnut Warlock stole her powers. I told them to stick their witch powers in their dusty you-know-wheres and I left, too. Not a chance in seven hells I was letting Stevie go off alone."

I still couldn't believe the ruling. I know the council's claim I didn't follow protocol was true, if not completely ludicrous. I did refuse to leave Peyton alone with his fears and his tyrannical father.

But to dismiss that disgusting piece of garbage after meting out a punishment so severe, from the *afterlife* no less? I was still blown away by Baba's disregard for my years of service with not an infraction in sight.

"This Baba Yaga, she's your ultimate…ruler? What do you call the leader of the witch world, anyway?"

"Misguided? Stupid? Meaner n' a snake cornered in a crawlspace?" Belfry quipped.

I tapped one of my familiar's ears, chiding him. "Knock it off, Belfry. Don't speak ill of her because she's essentially still *your* leader."

I didn't know what to think about Baba's stance. That she'd sent me away was so unlike her…

But that Belfry had chosen to stick by me meant more than he'd ever know. He'd left his world, his friends, his life behind the same way I did. But I was ever so grateful he'd jumped into my purse without my knowledge and come with.

"Anyway, yes, she leads our community. And while I disagree with her kicking me out of Paris ten thousand percent, I understand the pressure Peyton's mother put on her. I don't have to like it, but it wasn't as though I could have done much about it. Shunned means there's literally no way back in unless I become a witch again. It's sort of like an invisible fence I can't climb over."

"And you miss it?"

Closing my eyes, I nodded. "I miss my friends. I miss helping people on the other side the most, though. I miss it like I'd miss a limb. Anyhow, I left and came back here. I've never lived anywhere else—so choosing Ebenezer Falls felt right. But after yesterday, I'm thinking maybe Mars is the ticket."

Win barked a laugh, the vibe between us easing from intense to more relaxed. "Mars is bloody hot, Stevie. Besides, we made a deal. A deal you can't break because your strict code of ethics says you can't. As for the rest of it, I say bollocks. A pox on the loathsome lot of them!"

"Hear-hear to poxes!" Belfry cried.

"You don't need any of them, Stevie. You have a home and enough money for five lifetimes. So do you feel better for telling me?"

I actually did, and I couldn't help but tease Win because of it. "You know what would *really* make me feel better?"

"What's that?"

I smiled coyly. "Telling me how you died. Were you on a crotch-rocket, racing along an opening drawbridge trying to escape the bad arms dealer, saw an opening on a big oil tanker in the water ahead that turned out to be the *Exxon Valdez*, thought there was a slim chance you could stick the landing, but because your timing was totally off, you fell to your watery death in the Pacific Ocean?"

"My timing is never off," he offered dryly. Which meant, he wasn't going to tell me today. "Now, lovely lady, we brush ourselves off, pick ourselves up and get to the business we need to attend. We have to clear your good name and any further suspicion of wrongdoing, but more importantly, we have a killer to catch in order to free up your taco-buying privileges. So our first order of business? Connecting you with a lawyer I have on retainer, on the off chance Sardine comes looking for you again."

I giggled, rising from the seat, the heavy weight in my chest easing. "Sandwich. His name is Sandwich."

"Everything is a blur after mayonnaise and sardines and vomit."

"Speaking of Sandwich, he told me something interesting. I don't know if you heard, but he said Madam Z had been strangled."

"Wait! Shhh!" Win ordered, making me stand up straighter at the urgency in his tone. "Madam Zoltar! It's smashing to see you. You look lov— What's that, Madam Zoltar?"

There was a pause as the wind howled and the rain fell, one I strained into as I rigidly stood at attention while I waited for a communication from MZ.

Win made me jump when he blurted an astonished, "*Cluck-cluck?*"

"*What?*" I asked. "Are you hearing her right?"

"Madam Zoltar, have you been dipping into the wine? What do chickens have to do with this?"

"You have wine in the afterlife?" I asked.

"A buffet table, too. Quite an abundant spread, in fact," Win responded, and then he groaned. "She's off on a tangent again. I think she's well knackered."

I began to walk again with determination, this time directly across the street with the idea I'd head back to Madam Zoltar's and see if I could sneak my way in there somehow. I needed to look more thoroughly at the crime scene. I still didn't understand how Madam Zoltar had been electrocuted and strangled at the same time, sitting at her tarot card table.

My mind raced, replaying visions of the scene, but all I could recall was poor MZ on the floor.

"So what does a chicken have to do with any of this, do you suppose?"

"*Who?*" Win asked.

"A chicken," I repeated.

"Not you, Stevie. I'm still talking to Madam Zoltar. Say the name again, MZ," he encouraged.

Another long pause filled the air, making me wish I still had a way to communicate one on one with the spirit world. Everything was always so much easier if I could see an apparition's face and read their expression.

"Dan. She said Dan knows."

I stopped just as Madam Zoltar's store came into view, a frigid chill running up my spine, making the hair at the back of my neck stand on end. "Who's Dan and what does he know?"

Win groaned. "Aw, hell."

"*What?* Tell me! Who's Dan?"

"Dan is her son."

Chapter 9

"Crispin Alistair Winterbottom?"

"You're using my full name. As I recollect from my childhood, this is a parental tactic used to show one means business."

"*Shut. Up.* Shut up now. Stop reciting your spy DIY tips. I don't know if it escaped you, but I don't have a bungee cord I can repel down the back of the building with."

"Oh stop. Don't exaggerate. I didn't tell you to use a bungee cord to do anything. That's only for the skilled, and while the time will come when all my secrets will be revealed, you haven't earned your wings just yet. I said, dig a hairpin out of your purse to pick the lock, and make sure you use a tissue so you don't leave behind fingerprints on the doorknob."

I rolled my eyes, keeping them peeled in the alleyway behind Madam Z's. "And then you went on and on about types of locks and cylinders and torque or something. What's next? Lipstick machine guns?"

"Don't be ridiculous, Stevie. I never used a lipstick gun for anything. It's a pen. Ball point, to be precise, and if you're not ready for bungee cords, not a chance in all of my mother country would I allow you a pen gun at this stage of the game."

"That's not my point. My point is, shut up. All your gibberish about locks is making me nervous and confusing me. Now be a good lookout and cover me!"

I knelt down again and looked at the lock, forgetting Win's advice and remembering what Jo-Jo Swenson taught me in the sixth grade about breaking into my locker because I could never remember the combination. I jammed my hairpin into the lock and lifted, saying a small prayer.

The tension eased on the lock's pins and my hand twisted the doorknob with ease. "Hah!" I yelped triumphantly before covering my mouth and taking another furtive glance around.

I scooped Belfry from my purse and set him in the corner under the awning of Madam Z's back door, stroking his tiny head. We'd agreed prior to this break in, he'd be our lookout. He'd make the sound of a crow if trouble were afoot.

As I entered the dark store, Win was right behind me. "Do you have a to-do list?"

"Nope, but I'm considering writing up a kill list."

"You joke, but there's this list circulating in the Maldives as we speak—"

"Win! Can it!"

"I was merely going to suggest we add a tension wrench to your spy accessory kit to enhance your next lock-picking experience. No need to be so huffy."

"Listen, we're breaking the law here. I don't have clearance from Tom Cruise and his *Mission Impossible* posse to be in here. If we get caught, I get arrested. You get to float around and annoy me in my ear while you walk free, and I eat stale bread and creamed corn. So forgive me if I'm a little tense."

I picked my way through Madam Z's small living space, which was nothing more than a very basic studio apartment, careful not to disturb anything. The connecting door was ajar, and as I faced the room where Madam Zoltar had fallen out of her chair, I sucked in air before entering.

Forcing my feet to move, I eyed the fallen chair and the chalk outline of Madam Z.

The tarot cards hadn't been cleaned up either, so I stooped to get a better look at what Madam Zoltar had dealt while I wondered if she'd been in the middle of a reading when she died.

If she had, then the devil and death card could have some meaning. It caught my eye and made me wonder, if the cards were for a client reading, did it mean there was a devil mucking up their life? Or the client was the devil intent on death?

"Do the cards mean anything to you?" Win asked.

"Well, if she was doing a reading for someone, they're not good, but it also depends on the order she pulled them. Sometimes during a reading, you pull cards reflecting your own feelings. If that's the case here, she had a hint he was her killer." I stopped for a moment and gazed down at the corner of a card I was pretty sure was the King of Cups, but I couldn't get a good look at it without disturbing the order of the cards. "I think that's the King of Cups, which, if this was the client's reading, speaks of a family member bringing them to this point."

"But to the point of murder? Did she know she was going to die?"

I swallowed hard when I heard the evident distaste and upset in his question, and bit back my own disgust. "I don't know because they're such a jumble."

"So if this wasn't a client reading, then we can consider Dan or Liza as suspects. They're certainly family."

"It's a definite possibility. And see the competition card? That suggests someone who needs to be noticed. It represents brashness, someone who doesn't care who they anger."

"And the one to the right there—with the woman bound and blindfolded?"

"It's the card of a victim…" I whispered, surer than ever this reading had been for whoever killed Madam Z. "And the card with the cup, that represents relationships…and if I'm reading it from the killer's standpoint, he kills because the victim has what he wants."

"Which makes Dan a prime suspect," Win spat.

"Maybe, but what did MZ have that he wanted? The store? According to Liza, she had no money but her pension."

"We certainly need to talk to Liza."

I'd managed to find Dan's number in the phone book, but according to his dog-sitter, he and Liza were out of town in Tacoma due to a death in the family, and wouldn't be back until tomorrow. "Well, we can't do that until tomorrow when they come back from Tacoma."

I rose as I took in the scene again, including the scattered cards. "You know what I don't get? If MZ was strangled, what happened to her foot? If that hole in the ball of her foot was the point of entry, which is what I suspect, how did she electrocute herself like that? Did she step on a live wire?"

Win grunted low. "I'm just now remembering. Madam Zoltar had a pedal, almost like one you'd use to run a sewing machine. It was right under this table."

I looked to the floor, but the pedal Win mentioned was gone. "And what did she do with it?"

"The usual psychic fare. She used it to control the lights flickering on and off, move items and such."

"Okay, so then maybe it was an accident after all? Maybe the wiring was faulty."

"Or maybe someone tampered with the wiring. But if what Sandwich says is correct, strangulation was the cause of death—so the point is moot."

Win's voice had sailed across the room to an outlet on the wall next to the table. The white outlet plate was scorched, as was the wall itself.

Hands on my hips, I eyed the outlet. "Well, I'm no electrician. Any thoughts on how we'd even be able to tell someone tampered with it—or *why* they'd tamper with it?"

"Not a one. But after your explanation of the tarot cards and the talk of strangulation, it still means murder—by whichever means came first."

That's when I remembered the necklace. "Do you remember Liza mentioning a Senior Alert necklace she'd given Madam Z? She said they'd given it to her because she was keeping late hours here just to keep the place running. But I don't remember seeing it because she had a scarf on."

"I distinctly remember hearing Liza mention it, but I don't remember seeing it around her neck during any of our conversations. Of course, she did always wear a scarf. Maybe it was to hide the necklace. She mentioned a time or two how her family worried, and she did whatever she could to alleviate their worries while she went right on living her life out loud."

"You think she was embarrassed to wear it? Sort of like a babysitter she didn't want or need?"

"Wouldn't surprise me."

111

"So why wouldn't she press the dang thing?" I muttered, squatting down to look around the water cooler.

"That could be one of three things. One, if there was foul play, she didn't sense any danger from her assailant. Or two, someone took it to cover their tracks. Or three, she did press it, and the investigators have it in evidence. There's likely a chip inside that would have recorded a help signal when she pressed it."

"Or maybe she just didn't wear it at all. I'm more inclined to go with my first theory that Madam Z was a tough old bird and she didn't like the idea she needed help at all."

Win laughed softly. "You have the right impression. She was independent and funny and determined to make contact with the dead. She believed in the afterlife and ghosts and that's all there was to it."

My heart softened for this woman I'd never know, but who had stayed the course despite, I imagine, her fair share of mockery.

"Even though she'd never actually made an afterlife connection?"

"She confided something in me during the course of our conversations. It was the deciding factor in choosing her as a way to contact you—aside from the fact that she was wide open when it came to believing. Those are always the easiest people to contact."

His statement left me confused. "Then why didn't you just contact me directly? If anyone's wide open, it's a former medium."

"Because believe it or not, Miss Medium, you were like a firmly shut door. I'm assuming your troubles back home had soured you, closed you off or something. I couldn't get your attention no matter what I tried. And I did it all. Made scary ghost noises, flickered the lights, I even attempted a message on your hotel bathroom mirror."

That was a fair assessment of where my head was and sort of still is. I was heartsick at the idea I'd never be able to communicate with the dead again. It had been my way of life for so long, it felt like I'd lost an arm. It made sense I'd also lost my fine-tuning.

"So what did MZ confide in you that made you choose her?"

"Madam Zoltar said she knew it was wrong to give people the impression she really could talk to their dead relatives, and even take their money for it, but what she hoped they took away from a tarot card reading or séance was comfort. As in the case of Chester."

I smiled. "Forrest mentioned Chester and Madam Z spent a lot of time together."

"According to her, she would often check up on some of her customers in the hope she'd helped them move forward by telling them their loved ones would only rest easy if they began to live their lives to the fullest again. She picked up on small clues about the recently departed and she'd use those clues to convince her clients she'd made contact with the other side. Her heart truly was in the right place."

My chest tightened in guilt. I'd never thought too highly of non-witch psychics and mediums, as someone who really could make contact with the departed, but I guess I'd never looked at it from the angle Madam Z did.

"Also, something else worth mentioning. I offered her money, but she wanted nothing from me in the way of financial gain. She was just thrilled to talk to me—thrilled I was proof the afterlife existed. Now that I've heard Liza say she was struggling, I wish I could have done more."

The gentle admiration in Win's tone made me smile to myself. "You know, about that. What was the deal anyway? I mean, aside from doing some séances for her? Was she just going to knock on my hotel room door and tell me you'd come to her and asked her to change your will to my name as your sole beneficiary?"

Now his voice was sad. "She was going to make the deal with you for me."

I tilted my head as I looked around the disheveled room in thought. "How much time did you spend with her?"

"Only a few days before this happened. But I enjoyed every bloody minute. She was a good egg, Madam Z."

My heart clenched in reflexive sympathy. "So you were the first to find her. I'd forgotten about that in all the confusion. I'm sorry, Win."

His sigh was forlorn in my ear. "I showed up for our usual morning chat while she sipped her tea, and found her on the floor. That's when I ramped up my efforts to contact you through Belfry."

But now I was only half listening. Something had caught my eye. Dropping to my knees on the cold concrete floor, I peered under the water cooler's base. Using the tissue I'd used on the door handle, I wrapped it around my fingers and fished out the shiny object, giving it a closer look.

A pen. A brown and gold Montblanc pen. I held it up. "If Madam Z was on the verge of broke, why would she have an expensive pen like this?"

"It could be anyone's, Stevie. Maybe a customer's?"

I nodded my head. "Yep. Maybe. But I can tell you this. I don't know too many people in Ebenezer falls who can afford a Montblanc."

"I'm impressed, Mini-Spy. How did you know it was a Montblanc?"

"Someday, when I've recovered from unloading my last batch of baggage, ask me about my mother, Dita," I joked, tucking the pen in my purse, ensuring the tissue paper was still around it.

I wondered if I could get Sandwich to test it for fingerprints. If this was happening back in my heyday, I'd just read the pen's aura and find out whom it belonged to.

I rose and sighed. "Do you know if she kept a list of clients?"

He barked a laugh. "I don't know if you noticed, but Madam Z wasn't much for organization. Though, she did tell me she took lots of notes on clients."

A thrill of hope shot up my spine. "If we could find a list of her clientele, maybe we could begin ticking suspects off our list. Where do you suppose she kept something like that?"

"Your guess is as good as mine. I—"

"*Ca-caw ca-caw!*" Belfry made the call of a crow, our agreed-upon warning signal.

But rather than figure out how to get out of the store, or at least hide, I froze, my feet rooting to the spot. Oh, if Cagney and Lacey could see me now.

"*Ca-caw ca-caaaaw!*"

"Stevie!" Win urged. "Move it!"

"Where?" I whisper-yelled in my panic. "Where am I supposed to go?"

There were only two exits I knew of. The front door and the back. Oh, sweet Pete on a pogo stick, I was a goner.

"Ahem, people. I said *ca-caw ca-caw!*" Belfry's cry, urgently annoyed, sang through my ears.

"The bathroom, Stevie! There's a window. Go now!"

I made a break for it, hopping over the tarot cards and out to the front of the store, where I remembered seeing the door for the bathroom. Concentrating on not tripping over the candles and debris, I saw my target and made a break for it, throwing the door open and slipping inside.

My heart raced in my chest, so fast and furious, I was sure it would pop right out.

"Open the window above the sink," Win ordered briskly.

I looked up at the window, just over the pedestal sink, and my stomach fell to my feet. "Do you see the size of that window? I appreciate the thought, but no way is this butt pushing its way through that sliver of a window!"

The rectangular window—framed by peeling wood and covered in rain spatter on its frosty pane—was too small. Any attempt to get out through it would be like trying to push sausage back into its casing.

As footsteps approached, Win yelled in my ear, "Move it or learn to love creamed corn, Mini-Spy!"

My arms and legs decided to move all at once, tangling up while they tried to figure out which set of limbs should go first—upper or lower extremities. I fell forward, jamming my hip on the edge of the sink and knocking the soap dispenser to the floor.

"*Hello?*" someone called.

Catching a glimpse of myself in the mirror above the sink, my skin pale, my eyes wide, I was frozen in place again, my palms going clammy and sweaty.

But then Win was there, the warmth of his aura enveloping me. "Stevie, don't panic. Use your hands on the windowsill to haul yourself up onto the edges of the sink, and your feet to brace yourself when you get on top of it. Go!"

Win's instructions somehow soothed me, gave me focus, and I did exactly that. But there was still absolutely no way I was getting out of that window, no matter how much instruction he gave me.

As the rain pounded on the roof, making so much noise I almost couldn't hear myself think, I took the opportunity to ask, "Got any tips on how to lose fifteen pounds in two seconds?" I quipped, a bead of sweat now forming on my brow.

But he ignored me. "Pop it open, Stevie, and listen carefully. Feet first, flatten and elongate your body out as you go. Do it!"

I did as I was told, my hands shaking. I didn't even know where the window led. I just knew I had to get the heck out before whoever was in the store caught me and accused me of yet another crime, one I was definitely guilty of this time.

Jamming my legs out the window, I leaned back and fought a grunt as the top of the window sat on my stomach and the tracks dug into my butt, There wasn't a spare inch either way. I filled the entire space.

"I can't breathe!"

"Do you think breathing will be easier if the air comes from your prison cell?"

Fear spiked again. "You're not helping!"

"And you're not moving! Now slide out, Stevie. Spread your legs, use the heels of your boots to brace against the building, and your thigh muscles and arms and hands to inch you out and slide!"

"Did I mention I failed PE in school? Gravy, I was so bad. I couldn't even climb a rope without secretly using a spell," I said, on the verge of hysteria as I tried to feel for the side of the building with the heels of my work boots.

"Did I mention we're putting you into a rigorous training program the moment we wake on the morrow? Stop gabbing and get moving!"

117

"Did you just call me fat?"

"*Helllooo?*" the voice called again. A male voice, to be precise.

I heard the handle to the bathroom door rattle, my legs and stomach aching while I tried to gather the courage to slide as Win suggested.

"Stevie! You've got tops, maybe five seconds before you're caught. Yum-yum, creamed corn!"

I hate creamed corn. Hate it. Despise it. Wish it a thousand fiery deaths. Who knew it would be my catalyst to manage a death-defying leap from a window?

Engaging my last bit of strength, I stuffed my abundant backside through that tiny hole, using my hands to push as I gripped my purse, which still held the pen.

Just as I was about to launch myself forward, I vowed to hire a personal trainer with all that money Win gave me. A big, hunky muscly one who would help me downsize my butt while wearing Lycra bike shorts and a wife-beater.

"*Stevie, go!*"

I bit the inside of my cheek to keep from screaming and pushed myself out, stretching my body and straightening my arms so they cleared the window.

Eyes closed, I prepared for impact, wondering if I'd break a leg or maybe something far worse, like my back.

The dull thud of my work boots on the wet concrete and the spray of slimy mud, spattering my face and lips when I crumpled like a deflated plastic beach ball, made my eyes pop open to see how far I'd fallen.

I looked up from my puddle, frowning as the rain beat at my face.

"Well, well, Mini-Spy, don't be surprised if the people from the stunt double association call you up and hire you sight unseen," Win teased in that rich timbre of his.

Win's taunting laughter echoed in my ears because, as it turned out, my death-defying leap to freedom was only about a five-foot drop into the tiny, very muddy courtyard separating Madam Z's from the spice shop on the other side of her store.

I held up a finger and hissed under my breath, "If you say a single word, I'll turn that monstrosity of yours into a palace of pink and ruffles with glitter everywhere!"

Chapter 10

I hauled myself upward and dabbed at the mud on my face with my Hermes scarf, moving from the open window as quickly as I could before whoever was inside realized I was right beneath it.

I skedaddled around the corner and stood in front of the spice shop, turning my back to the street. Spitting the mud from my mouth, I opened my purse and whispered, "Belfry!"

His tiny white body came into view in seconds, swooping down against the wind until he was on my shoulder with a shake and a shiver before hopping inside my purse.

"What was the five-alarm fire about, Bel? Was it the police? Or a detective?" I asked him, still wondering about the guy in the trench coat I'd seen yesterday before Tito the Taco Vendor broke up with me.

"I dunno, Boss. But it was some guy who smelled real good. Didn't get a decent look at him because he had his head down and a slicker on. Dark suit and nice shoes, though."

"Maybe we should try and see who it was?" I peered toward Madam Zoltar's shop, the flashing sign no longer blinking cheerfully at me.

"He's already gone. He probably heard you carrying on about jumping out of a window and got spooked. Seeing as we have to wait to speak to Liza and her father, shall we continue this conversation back at the house before you catch your death?" Win suggested.

Ah, the house. I'd forgotten that was where I'd hang my hat tonight. "Because it's so warm and toasty there with no heat and no windows?"

Win chuckled that hearty gurgle of laughter. "You don't give my man enough credit. You'll see, naysayer."

I was almost afraid to put any credence in Win's words, but I was freezing and exhausted, so I played along as I waved down a cab and climbed in. My head was full of thoughts and a list of suspects as we left the main part of town and drove through the winding road leading to my new abode.

When we pulled up to the house, the cab driver turned around and hitched his jaw at the house. "Quite a project you're takin' on there."

I hooted a sarcastic laugh, handing him money. "Is that subtext for disaster?"

He grinned at me over his shoulder. "You know the lady who lived here? You a relative?"

I shook my head, interested in what he had to offer in the way of information about the house's prior owner. "No idea who she was. I sort of inherited it."

"Let's go, Stevie," Win muttered impatiently.

Clamping my fingers together behind my head, I gave him the universal sign for shut it and asked the cab driver, "Who lived here?"

"Some lady named Melinda. Don't know her last name or much about her. She died about five years ago, just a week after she bought the place. Fell off the cliff out there right into the Sound. It was for sale forever. Can't believe someone actually bought the dump. Thought she might be your relative."

"Nope. I had no idea who owned it. This was left to me by a really annoying uncle. You know, the kind who's a total know-it-all about every subject ever, but still loveable enough to tolerate over a turkey and a lot of whiskey on Thanksgiving?"

"You're despicable, Stevie Cartwright," Win murmured.

The cab driver winked a green eye. "I know the one. Got one myself. You have a good night now, and good luck with the reno."

I slid out and waved him off, picking my way up the steep incline to the steps. My feet sank into the soft mud almost up to my ankles. "First order of business, Spy Guy? A paved driveway."

"But it's so good for your abundant backside. Can you feel the burn, Stevie?" he ribbed.

As we approached the house, my breath hitched at the sight unfolding before me. How had this happened in the span of the seven hours I'd been gone?

There was already scaffolding along the second level where the bedrooms were located and long pieces of plywood lined the spot where the crooked, caving steps leading to the front porch once were.

The porch steps had a temporary railing made of two-by-fours attached to them, making it easier to cling as I avoided the pratfalls on my way up to the front door.

"I see my guy's here. Good show."

I looked at the big 4x4 truck parked down at the end of what I prayed was a driveway and pushed the door open, stepping into the entryway with a gasp. "Who is this guy?" I murmured.

"Only the best in the business. He did some incredible renovations for a friend. He's a bloody miracle worker."

"I'll say," I muttered as I looked into the previously debris-filled parlor, now cleared entirely. A fire glowed in the fireplace, and there was a lone wingback chair alongside the hearth with the once three-legged table propped up next to it.

Hammering from somewhere else in the house had me off to investigate.

"Hello?" I called, making my way out of the parlor and down the entryway hall to the kitchen—or what I'd secretly referred to as Nightmare on Samantha Lane.

As I rounded the corner, I caught sight of the alleged miracle worker, his overalls covered in sheetrock dust and paint, his dark hair sprouting from a Yankees cap as he studied the wall between the kitchen and the dining room.

Holding out my hand, I approached him from behind. "Hello? I'm Stevie Cartwright. You are?"

"The guy who's about to drain your bank account dry," he said in a heavy New York accent. Then he chuckled at his own joke. Dropping the hammer, he turned around and wiped his hand on the bib of his overalls, offering it to me. "Name's Enzo. Good to meet ya."

As we shook hands, I caught my first real glimpse of the kitchen. It was enormous, but gone were the cabinets falling off the walls and the avocado-colored fridge, now replaced with a small temporary fridge.

The countertops were completely wiped out, totally removed but for one where Enzo had covered it with more plywood and placed a shiny microwave and coffeepot. The windows on the opposite end of the room, tall and elegant, sprawled the wall from the base of the window seat to almost the top of the ceiling.

My heart melted when I saw the view. Mountains dipped in snow crested the dark purple and bruised-blue skyline; the Sound below them rose and fell in gray, choppy waves. In the summer, I imagined, there'd be colorful sails on boats, bobbing past me as I had my morning coffee while a warm summer breeze wafted in, and for the first time in a month or so, I smiled at the pleasurable peace the vision brought me.

Rejuvenated, I turned back to Enzo. "First, thank you for cleaning some of the debris out and getting the fireplace going. It almost felt like home when I walked in. Second, have you worked out estimates for me?"

Enzo nodded and pointed to the plywood countertop next to the microwave, where a ream of paper sat, before he went back to hammering out the wall between the kitchen and the formal dining room.

Surely he was kidding. I crossed the room and lifted the first page of the thick manifesto, where it listed a breakdown of the costs involved in renovating just the kitchen. My mouth fell open.

"Enzo?"

Without missing a beat, he grunted, "Uh-yup?"

"This can't be right." I held up the paper with the estimate for the kitchen.

"Nope. It's right." He went back to hammering as though I hadn't questioned his sanity.

"Your guy is a shyster, Winterbottom," I muttered, in case Win had decided to join me.

He gasped in that squealing way he used when mocking me. "How can you say that? Enzo's the best in the business. He's worth every penny."

"Of sixty thousand dollars?"

"Sculptures of David urinating coffee and champagne waterfalls cost the earth. Didn't you know that?"

I began furiously flipping through the pages to see just how much a fountain costs. "You are not putting a champagne waterfall in the kitchen. *Are you?*"

Was he?

"Why aren't I shocked to find a waterfall disturbs you far more than a coffee-urinating sculpture of David?"

"Because coffee is coffee and I don't care where it comes from."

Win snickered. "No. But I *am* putting in a state-of-the-art chef's package. It's not cheap to install a wood-fired pizza oven, you know."

"But I don't cook. I can't even make a Pop-Tart. So let's save some money and go on a cruise or something fun, huh?"

"But I *can* cook, and I can teach you."

A thought flashed through my mind at that point. Did Win think he could somehow get back to this plane to use a fancy chef's package? It made me stop and consider other angles he might have for giving me this house.

"But you don't need to cook. You can't eat."

"But you can."

My eyebrow lifted. "I thought after today, the idea was to lighten my wide load?"

"Your words, not mine. I think the view is just fine. I meant spy-training camp. I want to teach you some basics for protecting yourself."

My cheeks grew hot from his compliment, so I looked back at the endless list of work to be completed. "Okay, so care to explain the Italian marble countertops? Is that really necessary?"

"What, pray tell, do you have against Italian marble?"

"It's a ridiculous expense, Win."

"And you have a ridiculous amount of money. Enough for—"

"Five lifetimes. I know, I know. You know, I betcha you died bleeding to death from a paper cut while making it rain money." I swiped my fingers over my palm to show him what I meant.

He barked a laugh and again avoided the subject of his death. "We were talking Italian marble."

"Okay, if marble's your wish, so be it. I promised not to argue if you promised to let me pick the color of my bathroom. A deal's a deal. Now, I need to grab a shower, order a pizza, and talk out what we found today at MZ's. You up for that, Spy Guy? Because now more than ever, I want to know what happened to MZ."

"I'll meet you in the parlor. Let's hope Enzo got the water turned on and someone to sandblast the tub."

I glanced at the microwave clock and Enzo's back as he took swing after swing at the wall with his sledgehammer. "Isn't it time for him to knock off?"

"Enzo's an *arteest*, Stevie. You can't rush, or for that matter, halt the magic. It happens when it happens."

"What was I thinking? Of course sixty grand in kitchen renovations requires nothing short of an expensive magician."

I hauled the ream of paper under the crook of my arm and waved to Enzo, heading back to the parlor to get my purse and Belfry. "Meet you back here in an hour."

Plodding up the creaking, rotting stairs, I was almost afraid to see what I'd encounter on the landing, but true to Win's words, Enzo had come through.

If there'd been debris up here, it was gone now. It wasn't the Four Seasons, or even a Motel 6, but it was clean and there were lights. The wide landing spanning the second floor at the top of the stairs would be beautiful when done.

More tall windows overlooking the Sound lined the far wall, taking up almost the entire space, and though the paint was peeling and the floor had holes and were covered in dust, I knew it would be a space nothing short of spectacular.

There were two halls, one to my left and one to my right, where Win had generously told me to choose any room I liked. So I went to investigate to find the only one in the house that had a bathroom connected to it.

"Hey, Bel, you awake?"

"Are you kidding me? The dead are tossing and turning with all that racket coming from the kitchen."

"How are you feeling, pal? Warmer now?"

Belfry climbed out of my purse and flapped his wings, bringing him to my shoulder, where he nestled against my neck. "Yep, like brand new. So what's our next move, Boss?"

I crept down the hallway to the right, passing each room for a total of three. "I don't know, bud. I can't think until I take a shower. But I told Win we'd meet him back down in the parlor to reassess what we have so far."

Belfry grunted.

"What am I sensing here, Belfry? What's going on with you? You've been out of sorts all day."

"Gas. It's gas."

I stopped at the last bedroom, pushing the door open and smiling when I flipped on the light, which was nothing more than a stray bulb in the middle of the water-stained ceiling. Then I smiled harder.

Oh yeah, this was *my* room. Not only did it have a crumbling fireplace and another gorgeous view of the Sound from the front of the house, but it had that tub Win mentioned. I saw it from the corner of my eye, sitting smack in the middle of a bathroom the size of my old apartment back in Paris.

As promised, my suitcases and boxes had been delivered from the hotel room. I found them all sitting in a neat pile by the closet door.

Setting the ream of paper on the floor along with my purse, I scooped Belfry off my shoulder and plopped him in the palm of my hand. "Talk to me, old friend. What's the problem?"

"Is Winterbutt going to be your new sidekick? Do I need to start looking for another gig?"

I wrinkled my nose and tweaked his tiny yellow ear. "Are you kidding me? Who, in the history of all bird calls, could ever replace your crow squawk? You saved our hides back there."

"Being serious here, Stevie."

I knew this tone. He was jealous of Win and feeling displaced. "Buddy, I'd no sooner replace you than I would one of my limbs. You're in it to win it for as long as my human years allow. No way you're getting away from me. Yes, Win's a big part of that now, but sometimes we have to make sacrifices in order to survive. We needed a job and a place to live. He gave that to us in spades. And you have to admit; he's not horrible to have around. In fact, as I recall, in the beginning you were pretty smitten with his accent."

Belfry grumbled. "That was before he took charge of our lives."

"I get that he's sort of got us by the short hairs, but I don't believe he's bossy because he's a jerk. He's just a bossypants. I guess spies have to know how to take charge if they're taking down guys who want to blow the world up, right? Now c'mon, no more talk of us breaking up because I need this shower desperately. You're Sonny to my Cher. I got you, babe."

Stepping into the bathroom, I winced. There was a tub, sure enough. A rusty bucket that probably had once been a beautiful claw foot but was now spotted with corrosion.

Though, in Enzo's favor, there was a new shower curtain and showerhead.

But that wasn't all there was.

In the corner of this vast bathroom, with its endless torn linoleum flooring and ugly pink toilet and cracked sink, sat a variety of potted plants.

Belfry zoomed around the room with a squeak of excitement. "Did you do this for me?"

"I had nothing to do with it. It must be from your ex-boyfriend, Winterbutt. Maybe he wants to get back together?" I teased, noting fresh towels sat on the toilet seat.

"Okay, fine," Bel conceded. "He can stay. But just you remember who got you through the almost meteor crash of 2006."

"You were a real rock while I talked that warlock off the ledge, buddy," I said, blowing a kiss to him.

Cotton ball bats are notorious for snuggling together for warmth when they sleep—they typically do that beneath the leaves of a tropical plant in a tropical locale. Because Belfry was a loner, his plant/bed meant everything to him. It was like a slice of home.

On more than one occasion, I'd kicked myself for not taking Belfry's favorite plant bed with me when I was booted out of Paris.

But Win had taken care of that by providing every kind of broad-leaf plant he could manage, tucked into beautiful ceramic planters in gentle whites and a soft turquoise.

I don't know how he'd managed to get them here, and I don't know how he knew Bel really needed a boost, but he had.

That was all that mattered.

Chapter 11

"Stevie—time to wake up, Snugglebunny. The day awaits!"

I flapped a hand at my ear and the British invasion growling in it. "Go away. Do you have any idea how uncomfortable an air mattress is? I've had three hours of sleep total, Win."

Our meeting last night ran into a snafu when I was too tired to keep my eyes open. Win made himself scarce after showing me where Enzo had put the air mattress in order to let me get some sleep.

When I'd finally crawled into bed, I couldn't turn my brain off. If I wasn't trying to figure out who'd want to hurt a harmless fake medium and beloved town favorite, I was wondering what Win looked like. My Internet was spotty, so doing much research until I figured that out was difficult at best, especially with Win always nearby.

Was he harder like Tom Hardy or Daniel Craig? Or was he the suave Sean Connery/Roger Moore type? Or maybe I was glamorizing him altogether too much. Maybe he was a geek like Sheldon from *The Big Bang Theory*.

And then I thought maybe I just shouldn't worry about what he looked like because he would always be a voice—sometimes an interfering, annoying one, waking me up when I could barely prop my eyes open.

"We have people to see and things to do today. Up and at 'em. Also, you'll be glad to know your bed's being delivered this afternoon, along with a couch. Won't a couch be nice to sit by the fire?"

My head popped up as I spit my hair out of my mouth and rubbed my eyes. "You got me a bed? How did you arrange for a bed, and a couch, too? Are you off bribing more psychics to do your dirty work when I'm not looking?"

"Hah. You're funny, even in the early morning hours before coffee—which I understand is an addiction of yours. I most certainly did not bribe another psychic. I had a list of things I knew you'd need and Madam Z purchased them for me online just before she died, using my credit card. Oh, and I added your name to my credit cards as well. For life's little emergencies."

There was that twist of my heart in my chest again. His fondness for MZ was nothing short of endearing, and I wanted to find out who'd killed her because of it.

I sat up and forced my eyes to acknowledge the day from the wide expanse of windows, and the rain pounding against them. I'd missed the rain while living in Texas. Today somehow, it comforted me.

"So where are we at this morning?" I asked, jamming on my work boots to head toward the kitchen where coffee needed making.

"Today, Dan and Liza are expected back from Tacoma. We need to find a way to get them to talk to you, Stevie. You'll have to really lay on the charm."

I wandered into the kitchen to find coffee had already been brewed. Astonishment didn't stop me from sniffing the delicious odor of cinnamon and a dark roast. Did Win have the ability to touch things? Move them?

"Can you actually maneuver things on this plane?" That would be incredible, a feat very few spirits could accomplish.

"Not yet, beyond the newbie ghost tricks, but I'm working on it. Enzo made the coffee."

I tightened the hold around the neckline of my ratty T-shirt and looked around. "He's here?"

"He was. He's gone to pick up a delivery, but he'll be back soon."

"How did he get a key? He can't just wander in and out whenever he likes, Win. I'm a woman—primarily alone. Are you crazy?"

"You're a woman with a spy always on standby. And Enzo won't hurt you anyway. He's one hundred percent trustworthy. I told you, he's an artist. He comes and goes as he pleases, *when* he pleases. That's how he works. In fact, sometimes he'll be gone for days, looking for inspiration."

"In what? His hot dog at the Yankees game?" I found a clean ceramic mug sitting beside the coffeepot and filled it.

"Still as funny as you were five minutes ago. The agreement was—"

"I know, I know. All renovations have to be at your approval. I shut up and show up when necessary, no commentary from the snarky peanut gallery. But I never agreed not to tell you you're nuts for hiring someone who shows up when the moon is in its seventh sun."

"In the end, this will all be a memory we'll laugh over."

I wondered about this memory we'd laugh over. How long did Win intend to stay on the plane he currently wouldn't leave, and why? Was the restoration of this house that important to him that he wouldn't cross over? MZ's unresolved murder wasn't the only thing keeping him here.

"So another cryptic message from Madam Zoltar today," Win said, interrupting my thoughts.

My ears perked and my spine tingled. "Where is she? Is she okay?"

Win sighed, suggesting he was frustrated. "She's been floating about from plane to plane in a complete tizzy, but she keeps saying one thing. *Fish and chips*. I'd have to guess she's referring to me. I *am* British. It's one of the things that come to mind when you think about England."

"Cluck-cluck and fish and chips. Maybe this is some sort of food-related message? Maybe a chef killed her? What does this have to do with her son Dan?"

Win blew out a breath of air. "I don't know, but there's an obvious connection."

I shook my head, stumped. "None of this makes any sense. But I wish she'd cross over. Maybe then she'd find peace."

"I hope she will when we catch her killer. I'd like this special hell to end for her."

I leaned against the plywood counter and looked out at the stormy Puget, sipping my coffee. "About the end...gonna ask you one of those sensitive questions you get all uppity about."

"I don't get uppity."

"You do, and you get snappy and curt, but I'm going to ask anyway. Why don't *you* want to cross over, Win?"

He paused, and I thought surely I'd stepped in it, but then he said, "Because I like the in-between. There's no commitment here, but I understand what it's about. I don't, however, know what's on the other side. Maybe I won't like it. And seeing as no one's ever come back to tell us what it's like, I'm not willing to risk it."

Usually people lingered in the eternal waiting room for unfinished business reasons. My instincts said that had more to do with this than making a final commitment to cross.

"You do know you have to make a choice sometime, don't you?" I kept my tone accusation free, but that didn't seem to reach Win.

The air around me grew cool when he asked, "Do I? By whose authority?"

My finger shot up in the air. "There's that uppity thing. I was just asking a question. I suppose you could stay there forever, if that's what you want. I've never heard of anyone doing it, but go you for ignoring trends. You can stay in the in-between for as long as you'd like, Win. It's no skin off my nose. Now, I'm going to get dressed and then we'll see if we can't get Dan or Liza to talk to me."

I took my coffee and skedaddled out of the kitchen and up the stairs, unsure why it bothered me so much that Win wouldn't confide in me. He'd been in my life a total of two days now, and I was grateful for all he'd done, but I couldn't help the feeling in my gut—he was at war with his death.

Maybe he didn't handle it in the way Madam Z was handling it, but turmoil was present. Maybe it was about the woman who'd owned the house before him? Melinda?

We needed to get some Wi-Fi out here so I could scour the Internet when he wasn't looking. Until then, I had Dan and Liza to talk to.

I only hoped they'd talk to me, the rumored town murderer.

*****

"*You bought me a car?*" I was trying really hard to hold a grudge with Win after our conversation this morning, but he was making it almost impossible.

When I'd opened the front door to grab the paper, also delivered courtesy of Win, I saw the car at the end of what I hoped would turn into a driveway and wondered if Enzo had gone economy. But Win, in his own stiff-upper-lip way, informed me that cute little thing was all mine.

Back in Paris, I'd had a bike—which presented a problem when I'd decided to move across the country. And now I had a car. My own car.

"It was supposed to be here yesterday, but the dealership was delayed, or so that's what I gathered when I eavesdropped on the salesman reminding the delivery driver it would be fine if it was delivered a day late because there wasn't much I could do about it, seeing as I was dead. Little does he know what awaits him when he gets home tonight and reads my little message on his bathroom mirror written in the lipstick of his latest conquest."

I froze. "Wait. I thought you said you can't move things?" Oh, this could be bad. Very bad.

"I told you, I can't move-move things, but his girlfriend, the one he callously dumped, was easily manipulated and highly suggestible..."

Once I heard he couldn't move anything terribly important yet, I mostly stopped listening to everything Win was saying. I was too busy admiring my new car, my heart clenching in gratitude. I tucked my hair into the hood of my raincoat and gave my cute new red convertible Fiat the once over.

"It's in my favorite color, Win! How did you know what my favorite color is?"

"The afterlife enjoys a good gabfest. I thought I told you that? Or did you tell me?"

I couldn't stop grinning. "Who cares? You gave me a *car*, Win. Look, Bel, Win gave us a car! No more taxi rides, no more standing in the rain when the bus shelter is full, waiting for the bus."

Clicking the key fob, I unlocked it to the tune of a tiny chirp and climbed in, taking a deep sniff of the white and red interior. Then suddenly I was overwhelmed. Win's attention to detail astounded me, but his generosity blew me away.

Closing my eyes, I fought for composure as I gripped the steering wheel. "Thank you, Win. This was beyond generous. I don't know what to say other than you've thought of everything to make me comfortable, and I appreciate it. Say thank you, Bel."

"Thank you, Winterbutt. Oh, and thanks for my bed, too. Jolly good show on your part."

But Win didn't acknowledge our gratitude. He was all brisk business as usual. "You'll need transportation if you hope to pick up some of the items I need for the house. There are many trips to Seattle in your future. I couldn't let you squander your newfound fortune away on cab and bus fare, could I?"

I made a face and started the car, pressing the address I'd managed to find for Dan and Liza Martoni into the GPS system. "You just couldn't go with the warm-fuzzy, could you?"

"I'm unfamiliar with warm and/or fuzzy. Unless we're talking a cashmere coat on a Brazilian model. Now let's review, shall we?"

I pulled away from the curb and nodded, flipping on the heated seats. I had heated seats. Booyah! No way was Win going to spoil that for me. Not after a month in a flea-infested hotel room. I'd do that twenty times over for a cute car like this one.

"Okay, so here's what we have so far. MZ is dead from strangulation as confirmed by Sandwich. Neither Liza nor Dan is going to willingly talk to me because they probably think I murdered MZ, like everyone else does. We have two clues that make absolutely no sense à la MZ, via the strange and puzzling words cluck-cluck associated with her son Dan, and fish and chips. Forrest said he thought he heard a yelp when he was opening the coffee shop, but he wasn't sure if it was from the kids on their way to the bus stop just down the road or it actually came from MZ. The tarot cards suggest she was doing a reading for the person who killed her, but we can't say for sure because they were in a jumbled mess on the floor. Oh, and we still have no official time of death and the Senior Alert necklace is still bothering me. Our list of suspects is virtually nonexistent."

"Why are we ruling out your boyfriend?"

"My what?"

"Sherwood Forrest. We can't rule him out. We can't rule anyone out."

My eyes rolled. "His name is Forrest Sherwood, and don't be ridiculous. What's his motive to kill MZ?"

"Maybe Madam Zoltar gave him a reading he didn't like. Maybe she told him by the time he was forty he was going to look like Jabba the Hutt. In fact, maybe those tarot cards were for him."

"I'm going to ignore your petty behavior and move right along. Forrest would no sooner kill someone than I would wear anything Michael Kors."

"What do you have against Michael Kors?"

"I hated him on *Project Runway*. He was a total turd."

"Absolutely a valid, sane reason to rule out your boyfriend."

"He's not my boyfriend. Now quit interrupting. So, we still need to find a way to figure out if the police have MZ's Senior Alert necklace in evidence, or if she didn't wear it the day she was murdered, or if it even matters other than the fact that if she pressed the alert button, she knew she was in trouble. Also, we have that pen. The Montblanc. Why would MZ have an expensive pen like that? Did a customer drop it? Or did her killer? I think I should bring it to the police and demand they test it for fingerprints. The trouble is, how will I explain how I found it and they didn't? What kind of horse-and-pony show are they running, anyway?"

"It could be a crucial piece of evidence or it could be nothing. Let's set aside the pen for the moment," Win suggested.

"Oh and BTW, I got a voice mail from the Ebenezer Falls Police today. I have to have my lawyer meet me at the station at three sharp for more questioning. It's eight now. That gives us seven hours to grab coffee and question Dan and Liza. But I wouldn't count on lasting even seven minutes, with me as the interviewer. Because—presumed guilty before I've even been arrested. Oh, and last but not least, now that everyone in town suspects I'm a murderer, even my tragic love affair, Tito, make a note that tacos are off the menu for lunch."

"And Stevie has a date with Forrest tonight at seven, for dinner in town," Belfry added, settling on the heated seat with a happy sigh.

I blanched. I wasn't going to mention that. My personal life was mine. I think that was like rule number eighty-one in our handbook under the chapter What Stevie Will Do for Some Cash and What She Won't.

"Do you then?" Win said in that brisk manner he had when something was troubling him.

"I do." And that was all I was saying. Win didn't appear to like Forrest much, and that was fine. I did.

"As long as it doesn't interfere with our investigation, I hope you enjoy your meal. I'm sure Ebenezer Falls makes a delicious cheeseburger and fries."

Well, okay then. Someone was still angry with me, and a food snob to boot. Fine. Cold shoulder or not, I was determined to make today as pleasant as possible.

Because—convertible! Ain't nothin' gonna bring me down.

I pulled up to the Strange Brew, ignoring the sly glances and nudges people were giving each other when I hopped out with my head held high and entered the coffee shop.

There was the hushed ripple of awareness I seemed to bring with me wherever I went before the people in line and the surrounding tables turned their backs on me, dismissing my existence with chilly rejection.

Which was just fine. I didn't need Ebenezer Falls to love me, but boy would they be sorry when I caught the real murderer. I saw some apology casseroles in my future.

As I passed a table, the local newspaper was strewn across the surface with the headline: *Local Medium Strangled—Killer Still At Large*.

Closing my eyes, I took deep breaths before opening them and skimming the first paragraph of the story, which was all I needed to know. This was now officially a murder investigation—which meant that harmless questioning this afternoon was likely going to be more of an interrogation.

Squaring my shoulders, I went to the back of the line and squeezed in. I'd wait my turn for coffee and I'd do it with no guilt. I was not a murderer. Not, not, not.

"Well, if it ain't Ebenezer Falls's newest reason to gossip," Chester Sherwood chirped when he sidled up to me and nudged my shoulder with a wink.

I wiggled a finger at him and gave him a playfully admonishing look. "You know you had a hand in that, mister. In fact, as I recall, you were the first one to call me a murderer. Something about elephants and fandangos, right?"

He shrugged his shoulders and gave me a sheepish grin. "Aw, I was just lookin' out for my Tina. I overreacted. Lemme make it up to ya."

Tilting my head, I gave him a narrow-eyed gaze of skepticism. "What brought this on? Yesterday you were all 'Book 'em, Danno' and today you're singing 'We Are The World'?"

"The boy. He told me I should mind my manners, and he's right. Says he's takin' ya out tonight and he won't have his gramps callin' his date a killer. So whaddya want? It's on me."

I couldn't help but chuckle, giving his arm a squeeze at the mention of Forrest. "It's okay, Mr. Sherwood. I've got this. But thanks for the offer."

Chester clucked his tongue, his eyes dancing as he jammed his thumbs under his red suspenders. "Heard you bought that dump at the edge of town. Gonna have your hands full fixin' that up, I bet. Could have some nice gardens though, if someone were to take the time."

I wondered if I should tell anyone I didn't buy the house but rather I'd hit the afterlife lottery. I hadn't asked Win his feelings on it yet. "You garden?"

"You bet. Not so much nowadays, seein' as I live in an apartment above the store here, but I used to have a garden out back at my old place that was the talk of the town."

Gardening was my second passion after thrift store bargain hunting. If there was dirt, I wanted to be deep into it with a spade and some fertilizer. From there, an idea sprang forth.

"Do you think when we get closer to spring you might come out and consult with me? I'm an avid gardener, too, but I've never owned something so big with so much space to fill. I'd be so honored if you'd offer your opinion on landscaping."

Chester's cheeks went red. "You like hydrangeas?"

I grinned and nodded, excited by the prospect of growing the flowers I loved so much. "Lacecaps are my favorite. But I'm also partial to blue mopheads. I love them."

Somehow, I'd managed to impress Chester. It showed in his expression. "How 'bout roses?"

"Are you harassing Stevie, Gramps?" Forrest asked from behind, his warm voice sending a chill up along the nape of my neck as he cupped my elbow. "What did I tell you yesterday?"

Chester flapped a pudgy hand at him. "We were talkin' gardens, Slick. Relax already. I made nice just like I said I would."

Patting Chester's arm, I winked at him. "It's okay, Forrest. Your grandpa and I were just talking about the gardens I hope to create out at my new place."

"She bought that creepy dive out at the edge of town. Remember the one that lady—what was her name? Melissa Somethin'?—bought a few years back? Fell off the cliff a few days after she bought it. Daggone shame, that was. House on the market for years since."

That was the second mention of a woman owning the house before Win. My spine tingled with awareness. It was time for me to find out what happened to her and who she was.

"You bought that house? You like work, huh?" Forrest joked with a wink. "C'mon, I'll get your coffee for you pronto. You're gonna need it fast if you're taking on that project."

Win interrupting on the subject of the house only made me more curious. "Could we move this along, Stevie? We have suspects to interview."

Forrest attempted to usher me toward the front of the line, but I stopped him cold and muttered, "No way. I don't have enough trouble already? If I cut in this line, I'll be branded not only a murderer, but a cheat. I'll wait right here for my turn, thank you very much."

He grinned, his handsome face open and warm. "It's part of the perks of knowing the owner."

"But not such a perk if everyone hates my guts even harder than they already do. Now go make lattes. I'll see you at seven tonight. Meet you there." I smiled up at him and waved him off.

As he made his way toward the front of the store, I admired his broad back in a sky-blue knit shirt that hugged his lean but muscular frame.

I must have girly-sighed because Win was suddenly in my ear. "Aren't you the giver," he taunted.

My lips thinned into a line, but I'd forgotten my Bluetooth earpiece so I couldn't fight back, and Win knew as much.

"The perks of knowing the owner? *Of a coffee shop*? It's coffee, not diamonds, for bloody sake."

Tightening my grip on my purse, I balled my fist, hoping he'd see it. "Knock it off, Win…"

The woman in front of me in line turned and gave me the stink-eye. "I beg your pardon?"

"Oh! Not you… I'm mean, I said—"

"Aren't you the gal they're saying killed our Madam Zoltar?" Her squinty brown eyes lit up with fire and she squared her shoulders as though preparing for a fight. "What's the world coming to when a murderer walks free—and gets coffee on the house to boot?" she asked in a loud, nasally voice.

But my shoulders slumped when I gazed down at her. "I did *not* kill Madam Zoltar, and I am not getting free coffee. I'm perfectly happy to pay for my coffee."

But she wasn't done with me. Tightening the belt of her winter-white coat around her thick waist, she narrowed her gaze and wagged a finger under my nose, the ends of her flip hairdo bouncing in time with her finger point of shame.

"Don't you have a shred of decency? How could you wander around this town, parading all over the place in front of that poor child, Liza, like you're not a cold-blooded killer?"

Just as I was about to lose my temper, someone shouted from behind us, "Leave her alone! You're all so judgmental and mean! Stevie didn't kill my nana, Chicken-Opolis did!"

"Cluck-cluck," Win whispered.

Chapter 12

Pushing my way toward the front of the store, my eyes met Liza Martoni's with a question in them, but she turned and bolted out the door with a sob.

Good thing I wore my very practical running heels. I took off after her, darting from the store.

"Left! Go left, Stevie!" Win ordered.

But I didn't have to go far. Liza's sobs could be heard even over the light rain, coming from the direction of Madam Z's store.

"Liza!" I called. "Please don't run away." I edged toward her, avoiding puddles and holes.

When I made it to the front of the store, I saw the crime-scene tape was still in place. Shoot, I felt bad. Reaching for her arm, I squeezed it. "Liza? Come with me. Let's talk and you can tell me all about Chicken-Opolis."

She lifted her red head, her wide eyes brimming with tears. "Okay," she whispered, allowing me to take her hand.

I tucked it under my arm and pulled her toward the spice shop, where I hoped there was less of a crowd who wanted to tar and feather me, but where I'd also heard they served tea.

Pulling her inside, I was relieved to see there was only one patron. Amidst the shelves upon shelves of spices, I found a table in a quiet corner surrounded by the scent of sage and lavender and sat down.

Liza instantly let her face fall to her hands, tears dropping to the glistening wood table in salty blobs. Her slender shoulders sank inward beneath her neon-green hoodie. She looked so small, so defeated, I almost cried, too.

Clearing my throat, I kept my voice low. "Liza? I'm so sorry about your nana. But I'm trying to help find out who did this." I dug a tissue out of my purse, stroking Belfry's ear before handing it to her.

"Thank you," she murmured. "Every time I think I'm all dried up, the waterworks start again. I miss her so much."

My heart constricted. "Did you spend a lot of time with her?"

She bobbed her head, finally lifting her wide eyes to meet mine. "Every day almost. I go to the University of Washington, so I would always drop by the store on my way home from classes to be sure she had dinner. We never missed an episode of *The Blacklist*, and during the spring and summer, we always went to the farmers' market together."

"A college girl, huh? Bet she was proud of you, Liza."

"I'm the first in my family to go, and now…now she won't see me graduate this spring. She was so happy for me when I got in. She teased me all the time about how big my brains were."

"*Damn,*" Win muttered softly.

Yes. Damn.

"Did you ever notice anything suspicious going on with her? Anything that made you think she was acting out of character lately?"

"Not a single thing. She was in great spirits when I saw her the night before…before she…died." Liza worried her upper lip before pressing her fingers to her mouth.

"Any new people in her life, anyone strange at the store?"

"Just the usual suspects who came in for readings all the time." As Liza rattled off a few names of some regulars, I mentally tucked them away for future reference.

I reached out a hand in sympathy, squeezing her arm. "Liza, I know this is a really horrible time for you, but I want to help find who did this to your nana."

"But why? You didn't even know her. Is it because everyone in town is calling you a murderer? Ignore the bunch of gossips. They talk about anything and everything."

It wasn't just Win driving me anymore. It was Liza's grief. Her loss. I felt it, too. "No. The gossips don't concern me, but I feel this crazy connection to your nana that I can't quite explain. I'm the one who found her, and I've heard so many wonderful things about her, I just want to help. So do you mind if I ask you some more questions?"

She shrugged. "If you think it'll help, ask anything you want."

"What did you mean when you said Chicken-Opolis killed her?"

Now her eyes flashed hot and bright. "It was that man my father was talking to! Some guy named Hendrick Von Adams. He wanted to buy Nana's store and turn it into a franchise chicken place, but Nana said no. Who else would want to hurt her? Isn't money always the motive for murder? He could make a lot of money being the first in the franchise to open in the Pacific Northwest."

"So this Hendrick from Chicken-Opolis talked to your nana and she said no sale. Why did he go to your father then?"

"Because my dad is her only living relative besides me. He thought he could worm his way into Nana's good graces by using my dad. He kept telling Dad how dangerous it was for an elderly woman to be at the store so late at night, and wouldn't we all feel safer if she was home and tucked in with us? But he didn't know my nana. She was an active senior who always said she wasn't just going to quit living because of her age, and nobody could tell her otherwise."

I fought a smile. Despite MZ's fake credentials, I was sure we'd have been fast friends. "Okay, but to be fair, Liza, murder's a pretty big accusation because he couldn't buy a piece of real estate. What led you to say something like that?"

"The last time he tried talking my dad into getting Nana to sign over the store, my dad got angry and told Hendrick if he didn't quit bugging him, he'd call the police. Hendrick said he was going to do whatever it took to get the store, and that happened the day before Nana was killed."

I almost gasped, but I managed to keep it together as the waitress approached and I ordered us some mint tea in the hopes it would soothe the rattled Liza. "Did your father tell the police this?"

"We both did, and the police said they would look into it. But Hendrick Von Adams is a rich jerk with his fancy Bentley and fancier driver. He probably has big attorneys who can get him out of a jam in no time flat."

"Is he still here in Ebenezer Falls?"

"Yep. He's over at the B&B where my friend, Sally, works at the desk. She's says he's a total jerk, always complaining about the food and the temperature of the water. I bet it was him who killed her!"

I didn't want to upset her, but how likely was it this Hendrick guy had killed MZ? In the end, the store and the property would go to whomever she left it to in her will.

So I asked as much. "But if this man killed her, wouldn't he still lose the store anyway? Didn't your nana leave it to you or your dad, as her only living relatives?"

Liza's breathing hitched as another wave of fresh tears assaulted her. "Nana was going to lose the store in the next few months or so. Her loan was in default, and Hendrick Von Adams knew it! She had maybe six more months before the bank took everything. She kept telling us she was going to find a way to catch up, but there was no way she could do that. Not being as behind as she was. Maybe he didn't want to wait around for the bank to finally foreclose?"

And she'd refused Win's offer of money. She really did just love helping the bereaved. We could all learn a lesson from the esteemed MZ.

"Why wouldn't she take my money?" Win's question mirrored my thoughts, but his voice had an edge of sorrow.

"You know something, though?"

"What's that?" I asked, forcing myself to take small sips of the mint tea.

"The week before she died, she was really happy. Said she was having the time of her senior life. I'm glad, too," Liza said, her voice cracking. "I'm glad she was smiling and laughing again. Like really laughing. I think she had a boyfriend."

Or a generous spy friend who wasn't such a hardass after all.

I was glad to see Liza calming, her shoulders going from rigid to relaxed. As I gazed at her multiple piercings, that was when I remembered the Senior Alert necklace.

"Liza? Do you remember when you told me you'd given your nana a Senior Alert necklace? Do you know if she was she wearing it that day? Did she ever wear it?"

Her smile was a reflection of my emotions...sad. "She did wear it. All the time—because I asked her to. She wouldn't do it for Dad, but for me she did."

"And the police didn't find it at the store?"

"No, but Senior Alert was called. But they said someone called in after the alarm sounded and gave them the right password to call off the dogs."

I sat up straight. Who would know her password? My stomach sank. The obvious answer was a family member. But Liza didn't feel right. She was no killer, and unless she was up for an Academy Award for Best Portrayal of a Grieving Granddaughter, she wasn't lying.

Which left Dan. Ugh. Please don't let it be Dan. Liza would be left all alone without anyone, and I certainly wasn't going to ask her something so sensitive while she was in the height of her mourning.

Sipping at my tea, I tried not to wrinkle my nose—tea isn't my beverage of choice. "Did the police say who called in the password?"

Liza's lower lip trembled and her eyes filled again. "It was my nana. She called it in."

* * *

After I gave Liza my cell number, and made her promise she'd text me when she was home safely, I drove to a place I used to go as a kid, right by the Sound, and parked my cute little car.

But my heart was heavy. So heavy. Liza's grief-stricken tears, the love and friendships she'd shared with her grandmother, overwhelmed me.

Turning off the ignition, I leaned my forehead on the steering wheel and clenched my eyes tight.

"Stevie? How can I help?" Win asked, clear concern in his voice.

"Just let her get it all out, Winterbutt. She goes through this with everyone she's ever helped. She gets her emotions all stirred up, and because my Stevie's got a good soul, that heart of gold cracks a little when there's a person hurting the way Liza is," Bel offered, climbing along my arm until he was nestled against the warmth of the scarf around my neck.

He was right. I wouldn't go so far as to say I was empathic, but I've had my fair share of transference, and there was nothing I hated more than seeing suffering.

"I'm sorry, Win. I'm sorry this happened to her," was all I could manage right now.

Win's radiant warmth surrounded me, bringing with it calm.

"You did nothing wrong, Stevie. But whoever did will pay. If I have to summon a demon myself."

My head popped up. "Whoa there, Nellie. You can summon a demon? You didn't mention you could summon demons. Do not—I repeat—*do not* summon demons, Crispin Alistair Winterbottom! You don't know the havoc you can wreak and there'll be nothing I can do about it without my powers. Are you hearing me?"

"Duly noted. No demons. Are there any other horrific entities here I can summon in their stead?"

"*No!* Leave the dead alone, Win. Promise."

"Fine, fine. I'll leave the dead be. But by hook or by crook, I'll find a way to make this bastard suffer."

I let my head fall back on the headrest and blew out a breath. "Do you think the person who killed MZ made her call the Senior Alert people and give them her password so they wouldn't send someone out?" How awful. I couldn't bear it. My stomach turned again, somersaulting in a sea of too much mint tea and Enzo's coffee.

"I think anything's possible, Stevie."

"I guess this means it's an official murder investigation and that's probably why they're questioning me today."

"I wouldn't jump to conclusions about you being a suspect. What's your motive to murder Madam Zoltar? You have none. You stumbled upon her body and that's that. Don't worry, Stevie. That's what Luis Lipton's for."

Right. My fancy criminal defense attorney on retainer. The very idea I had to have one of those in my contacts list on my phone made me want to cringe. But if I had to have one, I was happy to take Win's advice. According to his stats, Lipton was the best in the Seattle area.

Gripping the steering wheel, I decided action was needed here. Talking with Liza left me more determined than ever to find this dreadful scourge of humanity and see justice was served.

"So next stop, the B&B? I want to sink my claws into that Von Adams dude and all his fancy money."

"Sounds like a plan."

I didn't think about how I was going to get Hendrick to talk to me. That never crossed my mind. What I wanted to do was put him in a headlock and make him tell me why he'd threaten an old woman who wanted nothing more than to keep active—feel alive.

A vision of the pointy heel of my shoe jammed in his ear came to mind. I'd make him talk to me whether he wanted to or not.

I made the short drive to Coraline Evans's B&B, The Sunshine Inn, and wondered if she even still owned it. Set picturesquely in a corner nook of the subdivision right next door to where I once lived, it was a staple for those tourists who couldn't afford the prices of Seattle, but still wanted to take day trips into the city or whale watch.

I loved its cottage-like exterior, the French Countryside appeal of the gardens and décor Coraline had devoted so many years to cultivating. In the spring, there'd be lilacs and lavender for days along the cobbled path to the periwinkle-blue front door.

Nothing about The Sunshine Inn said ocean or deep-sea fishing. There were no typical anchors and fishnets hanging from its walls, but by proxy, it represented Ebenezer Falls perfectly—quaint, small town, warm and cozy.

Parking in front of the circular drive, I noted the Bentley Liza had mentioned two cars ahead of mine.

Good, Chicken Man was apparently in. I hoped he liked unannounced visitors.

Dodging the pelting rain, I ran toward the arched door and pushed it open, stepping into the reception area. A cheerful young woman in her early twenties or so greeted me with a warm smile from behind an enormous reclaimed-wood registration desk.

"Welcome to The Sunshine Inn!"

Setting my purse on the rustic countertop, I smiled back. "I'm Stevie Cartwright, it's so nice to meet you. I'd like a little help with locating a guest of yours."

Instantly her pretty face shadowed. "I can't give out private information. The trust and privacy of our guests is our priority."

Holding up my hand, I nodded and smiled wider. I was prepared for this after Liza told me Chicken Man was a jerk. "I understand completely. But this is rather an emergency. I'm Hendrick Von Adams's personal assistant, and if I don't get some vital papers to him, well, I'm sure you know how he can be…" I tapped my purse and gave her the secret put-upon, minimum-wage-salary look—the universal sign for anyone who'd worked for or dealt with tyrants on a daily basis.

Her grin returned on her openly cheerful face, meaning, she got it. But still she shook her head. "He asked not to be disturbed by anyone, but you can leave the papers with me. I'll be sure to give them to him."

I patted my purse protectively. "I'm afraid I just can't do that—Sally, is it?" I glanced at her nametag and pretend-squinted. "You have no idea what he'll do to me if he doesn't get these. *No. Idea*," I emphasized with big, round, pleading eyes. "Could you possibly call up to his room?"

"Couldn't you call him on your cell?"

I let my shoulders sag in disappointment. "Can you believe I left it back in Seattle?" I used the heel of my hand to tap my forehead. "I can't believe I was such a knucklehead and forgot it, and if Mr. Von Adams finds out…well, I just hope my dog Belfry doesn't mind moving into a shelter. It's the only hope he has of getting that wheelchair he needs for his paralyzed back legs if I lose my job."

"Talk about going the extra mile," Win remarked.

Sally cracked a little. I saw it in her deep brown eyes as they melted at the mention of my fictitious dog. "I totally understand. I have three cats and I'd do just about anything for my furbabies. I can't call him. There are no phones in the rooms, but maybe I could just go up and tap on his door for you?"

I knew there were no phones in the rooms, or I had prayed things hadn't changed much in ten years, anyway.

"Would you? You'd save my life, and Belfry's. Wanna see a picture of him? Oh, he's so cute, all furry and—"

Sally flapped a hand upward and smiled sympathetically. "No need. I'll go do that. Be back in a jiffy." As Sally took her leave, heading up the narrow staircase toward the bedrooms, I patted myself on the back.

"A paralyzed dog, Stevie? Are there no lengths to which you won't go? Have you no shame?" Win asked, but I heard admiration in his whisper. "How did you know she was an animal lover?"

"Cat hair on the arm of her navy-blue shirt. Just so's ya know, Spy Guy, I've been around the block a time or two. I might not have been around Morocco's block or in some of the priciest art galleries in the world, but I did once stop a meteor from blowing up Boise."

"Not a lie," Belfry chirped.

Leaning over the desk, I found the logbook where I hoped it would list which room Hendrick was in and flipped through it. "Bingo!" I whispered as I skimmed the list of five bedrooms and located Hendrick Von Adams.

I looked around the daintily decorated sitting room just to the left of the reception area, in pastel blues and whites, with a crystal chandelier and vases full of dried lavender, and pointed to the archway.

"Now, if I remember correctly, if we go through the kitchen, there's a back staircase we can go up while Sally comes back down. Hopefully, Chicken Man wasn't too hard on her. But I promise to make it up to her if he is. A year's worth of cat food should do it."

Heading for the archway, I poked my head into the swinging door of the kitchen, making sure all was clear before scooting across the long expanse and raising a fist of triumph when I located the stairs.

Slipping off my shoes to keep my entrance quiet, I slid along the stairs until I reached the top, flattening myself against the wall just as Sally was heading back down the other set of steps toward the reception area.

"Coast is clear," Win called.

Blowing out a breath, I ran toward the Monet Room and threw my shoes back on then tapped on the door, wincing when it echoed along the wood-floored hallway.

"I thought I told you, I didn't want to be disturbed again and I have no assistant named Steven Whatever!" a voice bellowed from behind the door just as it popped open.

An angry man in an expensive Burberry polo sweater threw open the door, his hard face nothing short of enraged. He was all angles and chiseled and rock hard like a male model.

And then something clicked as he stood there, aghast someone else had the audacity to disturb him. He was wearing Burberry—just like the trench coat I'd seen at MZ's before the end of my love affair with Tito.

Wouldn't a guy like this own a Montblanc, too?

Was I in the presence of a killer? Was this Hendrick Von Adams the man who'd forced MZ to call off the Senior Alert people and then strangled her to death? Over some fried chicken?

"Who are you and what the hell do you want?" he all but howled in my face as he used his elbows to lean on the doorframe, looming over me like some Calvin Klein Gigantor.

"Stevie?" Win queried.

"Hmmm?" I murmured, leaning back away from the door as I fought to put a sentence together in my head.

"Very large, very angry man. Suggest new strategy. Copy?"

"Copy," I croaked before I turned to make a break for it.

But Hendrick grabbed me and whirled me around, his grip like a steel band on my arm. *"What do you want?"*

Wow, he was strong. Like, Godzilla strong. My instinct to zap him one came and went when, in that brief second, I realized I couldn't even if I wanted to.

Keeping my purse and Belfry close to my chest, I went limp as a wet noodle when he began to drag me into his room. Then when he least expected it, I stomped my very pointy heel on the bridge of his foot, grinding the spike into his flesh with a warrior cry.

I also noted, not only was he strong, but he had some set of lungs.

"Owwww!" he hollered, making my eardrums rattle, but he lost his grip on my arm.

With an opportunity to escape present, my heart pounding, my pulse racing, I made a break for the door, skidding around the corner and flying toward the stairs on the slippery polished floor.

"Stevie?"

The burly figure calling my name at the end of the hallway was like manna from heaven. "Sandwich! Help!" I screamed, barreling toward him, my ankles wobbling in my ridiculously high heels.

My feet somehow moved faster than my legs and I knew I was going to lose my footing before I did, but there was no stopping me as I tilted forward and rammed straight into Sandwich.

His enormous arms went around me just as the velocity of my body impacted his, making him lose his footing, too.

We fumbled and fell down the shallow stairs, me clinging to Sandwich's big frame, my mouth wide open and screaming with each tread we hit.

Landing with a thud, I flipped over him in an awkward somersault of limbs, where I landed sprawled out in a very unladylike manner, on the ceramic tile of the kitchen floor.

Win almost sounded exhilarated when he cheered, "Way to stick the landing! Good show!"

Chapter 13

Officer Nelson, with his disapproving glare and ultra-shiny shoes, was the first to offer me a hand up. "Miss Cartwright," he drawled in cool tones.

I allowed him to pull me upward, yanking my hand back and running it over my denim shrug, which was currently somewhere up around my ears. I straightened my clothing with an achy groan and caught my first glimpse of Sandwich's tangled limbs.

"Oh no!" I ran to the bottom of the steps where he was crumpled up, his head at an awkward angle against the wall. "Sandwich! Aw, sweet Pete! I'm *so* sorry! I was running from that deranged madman and I saw you too late! Let me get you a cold pack for your head."

I rose to go to the fridge to search for an icepack, but Sandwich grabbed my hand with a groan and pulled me to him. "Please. Just let me die in peace, Stevie."

"You're not going to die, silly. If you didn't die when you ate a sardine, mayo and sweet-pickle sandwich, you won't die from a little fall. Promise. Just let me get you some ice for your head, and we'll fix you right up."

I patted his wide chest as reassurance, but then old sourpuss Nelson was there, giving me the "could you be any more annoying" stare.

"Miss Cartwright? I suggest you let Officer Paddington have some room to breathe. Why don't you come with me and explain what you were doing upstairs at Mr. Von Adams's room?"

Instantly, I was indignant and huffy when I pointed toward the staircase. "Did you see what that deranged lunatic did to me? He attacked me for doing nothing more than knocking on his door! I'm going to file assault charges!"

"*Attacked you?*" Hendrick was suddenly in the kitchen with us, his expression still outraged, but mixed with some seriously obvious smug. He glared at me so hard, I thought surely my face would melt right off and slide to a puddle on the floor.

Jamming his hands into his equally expensive trousers, he narrowed his gaze in my direction.

But I narrowed mine in return. *Right back at ya, Chicken Man.* "You have some temper, don't you, Mr. Von Adams? Care to explain to the officers why you grabbed hold of my arm and dragged me into your room?"

"I did no such thing!" he openly lied.

Now I was livid. Like, so furious my eyeballs rolled so far to the back of my head, I was sure someone would have to knock my noggin to jar them back into place. "You did too!" I accused, shrugging off my denim jacket to show the imprint of his fingers on my upper arm. "I didn't do that to myself, did I?"

But Hendrick wasn't so easily intimidated. He came right back at me, his scowl cold and furious. "I told that pesky woman downstairs I didn't want to be disturbed! How *dare* you show up at my door unannounced?"

"Why so private, Mr. Von Adams? Just what are you hiding? Could it be the fact that you had something to do with Madam Zoltar's death?" I yelped, sarcasm seething in my tone.

"Oh, Stevie," Win groaned. "You've cocked it up now."

But I waved Win off like a fly circling a peach pie on the windowsill. "Care to explain this?" I yanked the Montblanc from my purse, still wrapped in the tissue like it was the Holy Grail, and held it up under his nose in ta-da-like fashion. "Does this belong to you, Mr. Chicken-Opolis-Moneybags?"

But Hendrick's face was completely blank. Which meant he was a good faker. I hoped. I mean, I had just accused him of murder.

Officer Nelson held up his hand, all calm and like a cucumber. "Now, Miss Cartwright, I'm going to have to ask you to take a deep breath and settle down."

"Settle down my eye! He certainly had motive to harm Madam Zoltar. Did you ask him about how he was trying to pressure her son into getting his mother to sell the store to him? *Did you?*"

Officer Nelson closed his eyes, likely asking whoever was in charge up there for patience, before he popped them back open and pointed to the parlor. "I'll ask one more time, Miss Cartwright. Please wait for me in the other room, or I'll be forced to cuff you."

"Cuff this!" I shouted up at him, but I inched my way out toward the parlor. Handcuffs weren't a part of my plans today. They'd mess up my date with Forrest.

I left the room with a squinty-eyed glare at Officer Nelson and Hendrick Von Jerk, just to let them know I meant business.

Huffing, I stopped at the reception desk, where Sally gave me stink-eye.

I openly sighed. "Okay, I'm sorry. I tricked you and I suck for doing it, but I really needed to talk to him. I just want to know who'd hurt Madam Zoltar. I just want to help."

I don't know why I was telling Sally my tale of woe—if it was a way of explaining my desperation or if I just needed a "poor baby."

"You don't have a paralyzed dog named Belfry, do you?"

My eyes fell to the floor in guilt. Sometimes, when I'm in the zone, I do whatever it takes to get the answer I want to hear, and collateral damage is inevitable. "No. No dog. But I've been accused of murder. So there's *that* hanging over my head."

Sally tapped my arm, her gaze softer. "Oh yeah. You're the lady everyone's calling a murderer."

Yeah. That's me. "I did *not* hurt Madam Zoltar."

Sally nodded her sandy-blonde head. "Oh, I totally believe you. I'd believe that creep did it before I'd ever consider you a suspect. He's so rude. Treats us all like we're his indentured slaves, barking orders, demanding we do all sorts of stuff."

Grrr. If I could only use my power one more time, I'd use it to whack that Hendrick so hard, his brain would spill out of his ears. But then a thought occurred to me.

"Do you know where he was when Madam Zoltar was killed? Was he here at the inn?"

She paused in thought then her eyes shone with disappointment. "You know, as much as I'd like him to spend a few centuries in jail, he really was here that morning. Up early, too. I remember because he was aggravated I'd spent so much time talking to the man who was checking out. But gosh, he smelled so good and he was so cute. He was chatting with me and looking for a place to grab some fish and chips, and I was recommending that amazing food truck next to Tito's, The Deep Sea Diver, all while Mr. Von Adams rolled his eyes and huffed at me."

Fish and chips…

"*Fish and chips!*" Win barked.

I tried to contain my excitement. This had to mean something. No way could fish and chips come up this often without it meaning something.

"Fish and chips? Yum! One of my favorites. There's a truck that serves them next to Tito's? How did I miss that?"

"He kind of comes and goes to avoid permit-violation fines. Guy who owns the truck's name is Jacob. He doesn't want to pay for the permit to have the truck parked. Sort of a rage-against-the-man kinda hipster dude. But if you know Marvin Wexler, from the town inspections office, you know what a by-the-book kind of guy *he* is. He's a total stickler for the rules. It's sorta become a joke to see how long Jacob can avoid Marvin before he catches him."

"Do you remember who the guy was that wanted the fish and chips? What his name was?"

Now she rolled her eyes at me. "Aw, c'mon. I think you know I can't tell you that. I'm already in enough trouble, don't you think?" She hitched her jaw toward the kitchen, where the police were still talking with Hendrick The Horror. "I can't afford to get fired, Miss Cartwright. I need this job, and Coraline's a great boss, but she's going to get some serious flack for what I did for you because you can bet your cute purse, that monster in there will make her miserable."

I gave her my best sad-panda face. "I get it. I just hope he wasn't the one to hurt Madam Zoltar, because that would be just awful. And the way things are going for me, I need all the suspects I can get. I figure it couldn't hurt to ask him a few questions, you know? Anyway, speaking of, you must be Liza's friend, right? She mentioned you worked here…"

Guilt shone brightly in Sally's eyes. "It's so awful what happened to her nana. She really was tight with her. Super close. Mrs. Martoni was a great lady. I feel so horrible"

"So do I. I had tea with Liza earlier and she was a total wreck." I sighed forlornly. "Anyway, it's fine. I understand your position. I just hope that guy had nothing to do with this. Whoever he is…"

Sally popped her lips then pulled me in, cupping her hand over her mouth. "Okay, listen. I can't tell you his name, but I think he said something about heading somewhere warmer with less rain. Oh, and he dressed really nice. The kind of guy who wears a fancy trench coat."

My spine tingled. A Burberry trench coat, perhaps?

I gripped her hand and squeezed it. "Thank you, Sally. You've been a huge help. I promise to make getting into hot water because of me worth your while."

For now, my head was swollen with whirring thoughts and theories. I needed to get back to the car and talk them out with Win.

Whirling around, I went for the door, but Officer Nelson, wet blanket award winner of the year, stopped me. "Miss Cartwright? In a rush to get somewhere?"

I gritted my teeth to keep from screaming. Turning, I pointed to my wrist as though I wore a watch. "Killing spree. I don't want to be late. Gotta run and set up the sacrificial table. It's tedious work to get everything right. Can we exchange pleasantries later?"

Officer Nelson actually smirked as though he were fighting a smile. Go figure. "I'll need to ask you about your side of the events with Mr. Von Adams."

"I've got an appointment with you guys at three today anyway. So it's a date. Gotta run, the chicken sacrifice waits for no one!"

I ran out the door to the tune of a low chuckle that definitely didn't belong to Win.

Jumping in my car, I threw the key in the ignition and headed toward the area of Jacob's fish-and-chips truck.

"And they say spies are manipulative," Win teased.

"Don't pile on. I'll already hate myself in the morning. Belfry? Do me a favor, take this down: Send Sally a year's worth of cat food and kitty litter."

"Got it, Boss."

Win chuckled. "So let's discuss. I assume we're on our way to the fish-and-chips food truck?"

"You bet we are. Maybe he'll remember the guy. I mean, maybe MZ was trying to tell us that this guy was staying with that Von Asshat at the inn? I still don't know what that has to do with her son Dan and what he supposedly knows, but I have this tingle in my gut we're on to something, Win. I don't know what, but it leads somewhere."

"I'd agree."

The rush of adrenaline I always felt when I was close to figuring something out coursed through my veins. "Oh! Something else, didn't Sally say he smelled really good? Belfry, remember you said whoever went into Madam Z's store while we were there smelled good, too? But we skedaddled because we thought it might be the police?"

Belfry hopped out of my purse and onto the seat. "Oh yeah. Whoever it was *did* smell good. Really good."

"And holy total recall!" I yelped, hitting my hand on the steering wheel. "I just remembered something else! When we went into Madam Z's the first time, I remember smelling perfume or cologne or something. It's what made me think she was somewhere in the store, but I didn't smell it anymore when we were near her body. I know there's a connection here. I just know it!"

Pulling up to the sidewalk where the food truck vendors were located, I put the car in park and jumped out in search of The Deep Sea Diver.

Tito was outside, under one of the tents set up to keep you dry as you ate, wiping down a table. I forgot all about our tiff and waved to him. "Tito!"

His glossy ebony head popped up, and then he realized it was me and his chubby, innocent face turned into a scowl. "Oh, no, no, no, *senorita*—ju no come to my truck! Ju bad, bad lady!"

Tito began to back away, but I held up my hand. "Tito, c'mon. Do I look like someone who'd murder a nice little old lady?"

His finger shot upward. "Ju might no look like bad lady, but bad ladies come in goat's clothes!"

I stopped advancing on him and frowned, letting my arms fall to my sides in defeat. "That's sheep's clothing, and okay. I understand. But can I ask you one small thing?"

He looked affronted, his eyes wide as he slapped the inside of his forearm. "Ju wanna know what kinda blood type I got?"

Okay, this murder accusation stuff was really getting out of hand. "Where's the guy with the fish and chips? Is he here today?"

Tito shooed me away, wiping his hands on his dirty white apron. "No! He bad like ju. Well, no as bad. He don' kill me. But he no like rules! Now go!"

I'm usually not so easily defeated, but if I haven't mentioned, I normally don't deal with the living when I help a spirit other than to pass on a message. I'd never been this personally involved or had this much hate thrown my way my entire time as a witch.

And it was beginning to get to me. Tears began to well in my eyes as I skirted the food truck patrons and headed back to my car, defeat a sharp pang in my gut.

I slid inside and turned the key in the ignition, gnawing the inside of my cheek to keep from crying as I pulled away, leaving Tito and his heated scowl in my rearview mirror.

"Aw, Stevie. Don't cry. I can't deal with you crying more than once a year at Christmas, when you make me watch all those stupid Hallmark movies. C'mon, Buckaroo, chin up," Belfry said softly, crawling from my purse to shimmy along my arm and settle on my shoulder.

"I'm sorry, Stevie. But I promise you, Tito will rue the day."

Sniffling, I shook my head. "I know I'm letting it get to me. But it's *Tito…*" My voice cracked. "He's the nicest man on the planet and he thinks I'm a hardcore killer. I don't know why that hurts so much, but it sure stings. I think I need to regroup. Just give me a few minutes at home to catch my breath before we have to meet Mr. Lipton at the police station, and I promise I'll be rarin' to go."

Win cleared his throat, his warm aura somehow warmer. "Take all the time you need, Stevie. You've had a rough morning."

As I drove down the road that took me to the house, I smiled my gratitude. Flying past the Sound, which normally brought me such joy, I all but ignored it, so caught up in what to do next.

Enzo's truck was at the bottom of the mudslide we called a driveway, the bed filled with two-by-fours. Well, that was something anyway. Maybe I'd actually have a wall to hang a picture on.

I slipped my heels off and pulled on my work boots, preparing to make the arduous climb to the front porch. I didn't say anything more—at this point, I was just too deflated. Though, the sight of the porch, and the holes now covered in protective plywood, did give me hope.

I pushed the door open to the tune of Tony Bennett and the sound of a drill. "It's just me, Enzo!" I yelled before kicking off my boots and heading up the staircase.

The drill stopped for a brief moment then returned to its droning. Trudging down the long hallway to my bedroom, the plan was to maybe grab a quick bath, relax before I had to attend my flaying at the police station.

When I rounded the corner, I stopped dead and gasped in surprise.

"Do you like it?" Win grumbled in my ear.

It was a bed. A bed every girl who likes a cozy nook to bury herself in dreams of. I almost couldn't move my feet into the room to approach it.

"Oh, Win," I whispered tearfully. "It's beautiful."

It was like nothing I'd ever seen before. Built directly into the wall where the windows faced the Sound, was the most amazing queen-size bed I'd ever seen. Fashioned like a huge window seat, the entrance was hexagon-shaped, framed with crisp white molding on top and edged on either side of the entry to the mattress with scrolled brackets. Beneath the bed, there were three drawers with matching scrollwork along the bottom.

As I approached and looked closer, I inhaled. Inside this heavenly creation where I'd rest my head was a plump mattress with a blue and white chintz comforter and tons of fluffy pillows to match. All around the interior of this peaceful nook, including around the white, thickly framed trio of windows, wainscoting had been installed and painted a pale lemon.

But the best part of this magnificent structure was the pure white bookcase directly above the headboard, built into the nook's wall and harboring one lone hydrangea and plenty of room for some of my favorite gardening books.

It was like coming home to a warm hug, and I didn't know how to say thank you.

"Enzo's got a stained-glass pane coming to place in the center window. But I hoped this would do for now."

"Do?" I squeaked, fighting more tears. "It's amazing. It's the most amazing thing anyone's ever done for me."

"Hey!" Belfry chimed from my shoulder. "Did you forget the Best Birthday Gift Ever of 2003?"

I giggled a watery sound. "How could I forget my Madonna tickets and neon-green scrunchie?"

"I'm rather sure I'll never be able to top that, Belfry," Win assured.

"Darn right you won't, Winterbutt. I'm going to catch a power nap, folks. Wake me when we're ready to take this guy down." Belfry slid from my shoulder and headed to the broad-leaf plants in the bathroom.

I sat at the edge of the bed and wiggled my toes. "Win, this was too kind of you. I don't know how you knew something like this would appeal to me, but it rocks."

"Bah. There was something about a vision board in your old apartment, an uncomfortable futon, the colors pale yellow and blue, and your love of the water. It was nothing, really."

He'd been talking to my spirits again. I didn't understand this man. One minute he was as brisk as a wintry wind, the next, warm as a tropical island. Complex and infuriating, delightful and considerate.

"Who made this in such a short time?"

"Enzo, of course. And his sons, Tomasso and Patritzio. They own a mill and woodworking shop here in Seattle. Beautiful place. Madam

Zoltar helped me find a picture from the description I had and she placed the order for me."

I grinned, hugging a pillow to my chest. "You were pretty sure I was going to take that deal, huh?"

"I was pretty certain I could talk you into it."

"I'm breathless. It's like you've thought of everything. Thank you, Win. This was just what I needed to put the wind back in my sails."

"You rest for a bit now. I'll make myself scarce," he said, and then his warm aura was gone.

Just as I lie back on the bed, there was a loud pounding on the front door.

Crap. Maybe it was someone helping Enzo?

I looked out the beautiful window to see who it was and my heart stopped. Why were the Ebenezer police here? I told Officer Nelson I'd answer all his questions about that stupidhead Hendrick when I went into the station for my interview.

Racing out of the room, I flew down the steps and threw open the door. "Didn't I tell you I'd answer your questions when I came in for my interview? You bunch are pushy, huh?"

Officer Nelson stood there, along with Officer Gorton, two other officers and some official-looking guy, who held up a piece of paper. "Miss Cartwright? We have a search warrant. Please step aside," Official Dude said.

But I wasn't budging. Enough was enough with the murder accusation. *"For what?"*

The official-looking guy gave me a hard glare, his bald head shiny under the light in the entryway. "Miss Cartwright, if you don't step aside, we'll have to arrest you for obstruction of justice."

I flung open the door and motioned them in. "Fine. I don't know what you're looking for, but have at it, boys. I wish you luck finding anything in this mess of sheetrock and rotted wood."

I stepped aside just as Enzo came wandering out of the kitchen, something shiny and oval dangling from between his fingers.

"Afternoon, Miss Cartwright. Found this on the kitchen counter by the microwave. Thought you mighta misplaced…"

Necklace? I hadn't even unpacked my jewelry.

Everyone stopped to look at what Enzo was holding, as did I.

And then everyone looked at me, their gazes hawk-eyed and hard.

Oh yay. Bet five bucks that was Madam Zoltar's Senior Alert necklace.

And right here in my own house, too.

Who'da thunk?

Chapter 14

"You have two choices, Stevie?" Win whispered in my ear as I stood by the staircase.

"Hmmm-mmm?" I muttered as the police milled about my house, yelling instructions to each other, tearing into walls and floors, searching with flashlights for something they refused to share with me.

"You'll need to use your thighs," he warned, his tone grave.

"Oh, good. Not a problem. I'll invoke the Gods of Pilates. I'm sure they'd be happy to help. Hang on just one sec while I dial them up. Oh, wait. I can't. Know why I can't? Because my hands are tied behind my back with zip ties, Win!"

"Then pay close attention," he ordered, excitement riddling his voice. "Here's what you do. Deep knee bend while you use your arms like a jump rope. Get your arms in front of you, lift them high, and bring them down as hard as you can, as quickly as you can. That should break the restraints. Then head for the windows in the parlor. Tuck just as you do a running launch against them; when you hear the glass shatter, roll. You'll have about twenty, maybe thirty seconds to do this before they take note and come after you."

"Is that all? Bah. That should be cake. I can't believe you don't want me to swing from the scaffolding into a half-gainer off the entryway wall as I somersault through the air, taking out cops like bowling pins as I go."

"Good point. Definitely a more solid stab at freedom. Do you think you can handle that? I'm not sure that's a level of escape you're ready for."

"Win?"

"Yes, Stevie?"

"Shut up," I warned, trying to keep my voice low. "I'm no more capable of making a jump rope of my arms than I am of winning the Kentucky Derby."

"No. I'd think you're too tall to be a jockey."

"Win!" I hissed. "Knock it off! We have a problem. How the heck did Madam Z's necklace get here inside the house? I've been framed, Winterbottom. Framed but good."

"Just like Roger Rabbit."

I grimaced as a cop raced past me up the stairs. "Not laughing, Win. I'm going to jail, pal. You'd better hope this Luis Lipton guy is good at what he does because I think bail's going to be involved."

"They have nothing to hold you on, Stevie. Nothing. It's going to take a lot more than a necklace to prove you killed Madam Z. If she was strangled, it certainly wasn't from something as flimsy as the chain on that necklace. And fret not; Luis will take meticulous care of you. I've made sure of it."

"I never did ask. How…?" I shook my head, already mentally answering the question about how Luis Lipton had been asked to take care of me. "Never mind. Madam Zoltar handled that, too, right?"

"Right. I put many things in motion before she was killed, all gambling on the fact that you'd accept my offer. Every rich woman needs a solid attorney. There are all sorts of unsavory people in this world, looking for ways to steal your money. It was a just-in-case plan. Thank bloody God, too, or I'm not sure where that giraffe would have ended up."

I made a face of outrage into the dimly lit entryway. "You bought me a giraffe?"

"Don't be ridiculous. I just wanted to gauge your emotional state."

"My emotional state is freaked out."

"Do not express any emotion one way or the other to these blokes. You are stone, Stevie Cartwright. Stone. In the meantime, what can I do to make you feel better as we pass the time?"

"Tell me how you died. No! Wait! Don't say anything. Just nod yes or no. Scratch that. Sorry. You can't nod. Just grunt if the answer is yes. I bet you died while you were hanging upside down in a dirty warehouse somewhere in like, Germany. You know, the kind with a lone light bulb swinging from the ceiling because of some unseen draft. I bet they were torturing you—you know, like maybe while upside down, your wrists cuffed, your fingers were hanging in a dirty puddle of water and they used jumper cables to shock you into telling them where the diamonds were. Am I close?"

"Jumper cables are so old-spy torture."

But I'd lost my zeal for guessing how he'd died. As more of the officers centered in on the crumbling dining room, talking and pointing, I had to wonder what else might have been planted and by whom.

"What do you suppose they're looking for? I mean, if the murder weapon was her scarf, what's left?"

"I don't know. Your diabolical plan drawn on paper, perhaps? Local law enforcement is below my pay grade. I'm used to espionage and intrigue. It's bigger, more complex, messier than just plain old small-town murder."

"Well, la-dee-da. You're so fancy," I said with an eye roll.

"I'm just stating the facts. When I'm in the height of a mission, I'm looking for codes for bombs and Russian submarine navigational longitudes and latitudes. But I'll learn to simplify."

Leaning back as another police officer took off up the stairs, I fought a tremble in my voice and said, "Do me a favor. Make sure Belfry calls this Luis Lipton to be sure he doesn't miss our meeting at three. I have a feeling he's more necessary than ever. You stay here. It's too much with you in my ear when I need to concentrate, and if Luis is as good as you say he is, I won't have to say much anyway. Plus, Bel's never very good without me. He's a smart aleck, but he's a sensitive one. Also, tell Bel to stay put. No matter what, he doesn't leave the house, okay? I want him safe, not locked up in some evidence locker. You'll look after him, won't you?"

"Of course, but Lipton's, as you Americans say, a shark. He'll have you out in no time. Belfry will hardly know you're gone. I give you my word."

Officer Nelson approached me, his tall frame dwarfing mine. "Miss Cartwright, please come with me."

I smiled coyly at him. "Are we going for a ride in your shiny cruiser? Will you turn the lights and sirens on?"

"No."

"Aw, you're no fun. Sandwich...er, I mean, Officer Paddington offered to the last time I was needlessly taken to your place of business. You could learn a thing or two from him. He's super easygoing. You, on the other hand? So tense, rigid even. Ease up there, Cowpoke. You'll get wrinkles."

Lifting his clean-shaven chin, Officer Nelson pointed toward my front door. "After you."

Okay, obviously the good times weren't rolling with Officer Nelson anymore. I had a glimmer of hope he considered me innocent back at the inn, but now he looked like he was pretty sure I was involved. Who *wouldn't* think I was somehow involved when I had Madam Z's necklace?

So I did as I was told. Even I knew when to shut up. Well, mostly. As I descended the stairs with the aide of Officer Detached, my stomach twisted and turned in anxious, empty turmoil.

"Stay tough, Stevie. I'm on it. And if they break out the jumper cables, remember to clench your teeth. It makes the pain easier to withstand. Don't ever let 'em see you sweat!" Win called behind me.

Yeah, yeah. Easy for Spy Guy to say. He could jump rope with his arms.

* * *

I sat in the interrogation room of my hometown police station under the most heinous of glaring fluorescent lights beside my swanky lawyer, Luis Lipton, in his seven-hundred-dollar-an-hour pinstriped gray suit, and stared down the detective across from me.

Oddly, the players were a lot like they were on TV.

There was the first detective; he was Good Cop, according to Luis. Detective Ward Montgomery, early forties, nice enough suit on a detective's salary, easy enough on the eyes, calm, obvious stabs at endearing himself to me, chummy even.

"So am I right when I'm hearing you say you have no idea how Tina Martoni's Senior Alert necklace ended up at your house, yet an anonymous tip led us straight to it?" he coaxed, pretending interest in my every word by sitting his chin on his hand and smiling.

Yeah. That was how they'd discovered the necklace was at my house. An anonymous tip...

I nodded and kept my answers simple, just like Luis told me to do as he prepped me for my interview and right after he made Bad Cop remove my zip-tie restraints. "You're correct."

"Well, how can that be, Stevie? Don't you know what's in your own house? It was pretty empty—not much in the way of anything to speak of. Your contractor said he found the necklace on the counter. How could you miss it if you weren't the one who put it there in the first place?" he asked in a friendly tone.

But Luis held up a hand, setting his glasses at the end of his long nose and peering over them at Good Cop. "I believe this has been asked and answered, Detective. Your redundancy has become quite tedious. Now, you clearly have no solid evidence against my client. There's no physical evidence except my client's muddy footprints in the store, which we've very clearly explained. You have nothing more than a necklace with—I'm going to guess, once the lab results return—no DNA from Miss Cartwright."

Now, Bad Cop? He was wired for sound. Like he'd had too many Red Bulls in a row.

Bad Cop was rather a mashup of Andy Sipowicz from *NYPD Blue*, all hard and rabid yelling, mixed with Ice-T on *Law & Order: SVU*, intense and quietly thinking of multiple ways to crush my skull with his bare hands while he chewed gum with endless pops and crackles.

Bad Cop's name was Detective Sean Moore. He dressed like he was trying to prove he was one of the people, just a normal citizen in low-slung jeans and a black T-shirt accentuating his crazy mass of muscles, and he'd been alternately yelling at me for over an hour while Detective Montgomery watched, swooping in when soothing me appeared necessary.

Detective Moore drove his fist against the metal table, making me jump from my musings. "You forced that poor little old lady to call off those Senior Alert people then you thanked her by killing her, didn't you? Wrapped that scarf around her neck so hard and pulled so tight, she hit that hocus-pocus pedal of hers with her foot and electrocuted herself!" he hollered in my face.

I blinked at him and his blotchy red face and sweat-beaded brow in silent awe. Phew. Bet his blood pressure was sky-high. But I was glad I finally had an explanation for the hole in Madam Zoltar's foot, which, according to Luis and the preliminary coroner's reports, was almost definitely not the cause of death and nothing more than a bizarre coincidence.

Though, when Luis told me to remain expressionless no matter what the Dynamic Duo did or said, he didn't mention how upsetting it would be to hear Madam Z's death revealed in actual words. I had to fight to keep from cracking by digging my nails into my palms.

"Didn't you just come into a large amount of cash, Stevie?" Detective Montgomery crooned.

"Having money is certainly not a crime. What's your point, Detective?" Luis asked as he adjusted his cufflinks, his piercing gaze making even *me* shrink.

"Mayyybe our Stevie here wanted to buy Tina Martoni's store? Maybe she wanted to buy it so bad, that when Tina Martoni wouldn't give it up, she *made* her give it up? Tina Martoni was in a lot of debt. Having money has its privileges, doesn't it, Stevie? Sometimes it can make you think you deserve to take something that isn't yours..." Detective Moore drawled as though he were the cleverest of us all.

Yeah, I felt so privileged today. Being called a murderer by everyone, including your favorite taco vendor, has privilege written all over it.

Luis cocked his slick salt-and-pepper head with a sharp right. "And what do you suppose she wanted to use this store for once she got her hands on it, Detective Moore? If you check with the attorney who handled the will, as any skilled detective worth his weight in taxpayer money would, you'll find she didn't know about the inheritance or that she was a sole beneficiary until later in the day *after* Mrs. Martoni was killed. And how does this suddenly remove Mr. Von Adams from suspicion? Didn't he want to purchase the store, too?"

Yeah. What he said.

Detective Moore's face flinched a little, his jaw tightening when Luis poked a hole in his outlandish theory. "He didn't have a Senior Alert necklace in his room at the inn. And that doesn't mean Miss Cartwright here didn't have her eye on the store before she got all that cash. Maybe she knew she was gonna get it?"

Luis cleared his throat and folded his hands in front of him on the cold table. "Gentleman? You do realize you're just stalling for time? Miss Cartwright isn't a viable suspect. I think we all know as much. She has no motive. Her record is clean as a whistle. She's only just returned to town a month ago, and has never been seen in or around Tina Martoni's place of business until two days ago—the day of the murder."

Had it only been two days? It felt like two million years.

As Luis continued, he set a package of papers in his briefcase and snapped it shut. "I don't know what you think you can charge her with at this point, but whatever it is, I'm sure I can crush the charge in a matter of moments. Now, I have a dinner date with my mother for, of all things, cabbage rolls and some riveting Game Show Network television. Miss Cartwright has to go home and hire a cleaning crew to dig herself out of your department's careless disregard for her personal belongings. I believe we're done."

He rose, smoothing his silk blue tie over his firm stomach before buttoning his suit jacket and looking at both detectives with that unblinking stare. "Good day to you both. Please feel free to contact my client via *me* when you have evidence worthy of my seven-hundred-dollar-an-hour fee. I'll show up again for nothing less than proof *bigger* than an anonymous phone call and a necklace so blatantly planted at my client's house."

Holding out his hand, Luis pulled me up from my chair and held the door to the interview room open for me.

As childish as this sounds, I wanted to turn around and stick my tongue out at them, or at the very least give them a more NC-17-rated middle finger, but I was exhausted.

Really what I wanted to do was just go home, curl up in the amazing bed Win had given me and close my eyes, forgetting today ever happened.

Out in the reception area of the station, I saw Sandwich, hobbling around on crutches. Without thinking, I approached him with the intent to apologize.

My hands outstretched, I murmured, "Oh, Sand...er, Lyn. I'm so sorry. This happened because of me, didn't it?" I pointed to his foot, wrapped in an ACE bandage.

But Sandwich held up a wide hand to stop me, his always pleasant face tight and withdrawn. "You stay right where you are, Stevie. I'm already in enough trouble because of you and I can't say anything more. So I'll thank ya kindly to keep your distance."

I don't know if it was Sandwich losing faith in me, or the fact that the two detectives were standing outside the interview room, arms crossed over their chests, watching me as though I were a puppy killer, but I was done in.

Just over all of it.

Luis saved me from making a scene by crying in front of everyone when he put his hand at my elbow and led me out of the station to his car, where he helped me in and drove me home as I fought tears.

I was no closer to catching this killer, Madam Zoltar's spirit was in total turmoil and now one of the few people in town who actually didn't hate me wanted nothing to do with me.

And I couldn't even drown my sorrows in Tito's tacos because he hated me, too.

Boo-hiss.

Chapter 15

"Steeeevie! Come now. Don't be sad."

"Me, sad? Don't be silly, Win," I said, my voice muffled from beneath the pillow. "What's there to be sad about? That I've been framed for murder? That we might never find out who killed Madam Zoltar? Or that a killer is running free and getting away with said murder? Don't talk crazy. We should have a party. Maybe some balloons and a cake, too."

"Want me to tell you how I died?" Win singsonged the question in my ear.

I didn't even budge. No way was I taking that bait. "Not interested."

"Not true."

I pushed the pillow off my face and sighed. "Maybe it isn't. Or maybe I've decided I'd rather you *want* to tell me versus share your story as a bribe. But know this, Crispin Alistair Winterbottom, when you tell me, it'll mean we've crossed a milestone—it'll mean you finally trust me."

Win blustered. "I do trust you now. I gave you millions of dollars in spy money and my beloved house. How much more trust is there?"

I rolled to my side and looked out the windows inside my little nook of a bed. "Those are all superficial things, Win. Things you couldn't use yourself now even if you wanted to. You could have given them to anyone. They have nothing to do with friendship."

I can't say why I was picking a fight with Win, other than I was angry all over. Maybe bruised was a better word. It wasn't like me to give in to feeling sorry for myself, but tonight, without my powers, with the possibility of jail time looming in my future, bruised was the best word I could find to sum up how I was feeling. Maybe I needed Win to trust me because no one else did.

Belfry's tiny hands pulled him up along my body until he was at my ear. "Cheer up, Stevie. We ordered pizzzaaaa," he enticed.

"Oh, nice. Gobs of cheese and pepperoni will make a killer running free so much easier to digest."

Win made a funny gagging noise from his throat. "No pepperoni. That's for heathens. Olives and sausage with plump Roma tomatoes make a pizza, Stevie. Anyone with taste buds knows that."

I sat up, taking Bel with me. "It doesn't matter. I'm not hungry anyway. I can't eat while there's a murderer out there, Win. And what the heck did Madam Z mean when she mentioned Dan knew? She said cluck-cluck and Dan knows."

"She did. Maybe she's just disoriented at this point. Maybe she's throwing out words relating to what troubled her before she died. Obviously, Von Adams met with Dan. We know that. Or maybe she threw those key words out there to get us to the inn?"

"According to Luis, Chicken-Man has an alibi. So, if it's not Hendrick Von Adams then it has to be the fish-and-chips guy. I feel it. I mean, who else is left except for Dan? The only person we haven't questioned. But he doesn't feel right, yanno?"

"I do know," Win answered.

"So this fish-and-chips guy… W*ho* is he?" I asked more to myself than anyone else as I climbed out of the bed and slid to the floor, dropping into my discarded work boots.

Thankfully, the police hadn't torn up my new bed—much. I'd expected to find stuffing from my pillows from one end of the room to the other, but it had been mostly untouched.

They had, however, rifled through all my suitcases.

"Tell me what Luis said and where we're at right now."

I grabbed my robe and slid into it, fighting the chilly memory the police station brought. "He said there was absolutely no reason to panic and he'd eat his own shoes if they actually came up with something solid to convince a judge to lock me up. I told him that I hoped he had soft shoes, the way my luck's been going. He laughed, which, BTW, I didn't think he was capable of because he's crazy serious and that glare he has is intimidating as all get out. Anyway, he told me to lay low, don't leave town, the norm, and not to worry. But this changes nothing as far as I'm concerned. Someone got away with murdering MZ and is trying to frame me for it. I can't live with that, Win. I have to find whoever did this."

Win's voice followed me as I made my way down the stairs, stepping over and around the various loose boards. "That's the spirit. A much better attitude! Now, you need to eat. You haven't had anything since breakfast. Once we have some food in you, we'll hash out what we discovered today."

I wandered down the hallway, stepping around the table saw by the wall of the stairs and headed to the kitchen, fumbling around for a light, still unclear of the house's layout. When I flicked the switch, I inhaled.

"Is Enzo a magician?" I asked, amazed at his progress. The entire wall into the dining room had been knocked out, all the old flooring was now gone, leaving the space even more open and airy.

The windows facing the Sound, eight in total, were trimmed in the same thick wood that was in my nook bed, and an unpainted window seat sat enticingly beneath the middle three windows.

A design for the layout of the cabinets and appliances was sitting by the microwave, waiting for my approval, but I couldn't absorb it all right now.

I made my way to the tiny fridge Enzo had brought in and grabbed a bottled water, staring out into the dark night.

"So do you like the layout of the kitchen, Stevie?" Win finally asked.

I shrugged my shoulders. "Sure. It looks like it should be easy enough to find a place for my Pop-Tarts and crunchy peanut butter with all those cabinets."

"There's just no educating you, is there?"

Chuckling, I shook my head. "I told you, I don't cook. I don't want to learn to cook. I can just as easily order in or eat cereal."

"Speaking of your underdeveloped taste buds and food for ten-year-olds, didn't you have a date with Sherwood Forrest tonight?"

Remorse tweaked me. "I did, but I canceled. First, I don't want to subject him to the kind of treatment I've been getting around town lately. Second, my heart's not in it. I can't think of anything else until we at least get a lead on fish-and-chips guy. So I texted him and asked for a rain check. Though, if I were him, I wouldn't want to go anywhere with me."

There was a loud knock at the door, thwarting more conversation about Forrest. I set Belfry on the counter on a hand towel. "You wait here. I'll be back to get your dinner."

Though I was feeling pretty blue, the thought of some food did cheer me up. My stomach was a sea of acid from nothing but liquids today.

The light to the front porch didn't work yet, so I couldn't see very well. But seriously, who'd haul themselves up that steep, muddy incline but a teenager who might get a tip out of it?

Well, except for maybe the local police. They'd had no trouble at all hunting me down.

"Who is it?" I called more out of habit than anything else.

"Pizza man!"

His silhouette behind the warped front door said he was indeed the pizza man, judging by his signature hat and the big square box.

My stomach grumbled as I flung the door open, turning to look for my purse so I could give him a big tip for coming all the way to the front door of Mayhem Manor without chickening out.

"C'mon in," I said over my shoulder as I located my purse on the banister of the steps. "Lemme just grab you some money. Listen, thanks for coming all the way up here. I know it's a hike in all that mud, especially in the dark. But there's a big tip in this for—"

"Fish and chips, Stevie!" Win bellowed. "Bloody hell, fish and chips!"

I was just about to tell Spy Guy to shut it about the fish-and-chips guy until the pizza-delivery kid was gone, but I didn't have the chance before the sharp sting of something with a blunt edge whacked me on the back of my head.

* * *

As my brain found its way back to the surface, and words in my ear strung together, I fought to open my eyes, the throb in my head a staccato rhythm.

"Stevie! Wake up, damn it. You must wake up! Where's your phone?" And then he hissed, "Damn! He smashed it."

My groan was long and pained. "What the heck happened?" I managed to push the words from my lips as I realized I was tied up.

The sticky residue of duct tape pulled at the skin around my wrists and the chafing of rope around my ankles itched.

Now my eyes popped right open to discover I was in the basement of Mayhem Manor. Smack in the middle of the room, which spanned the entire house. Nothing but me and a bazillion cobwebs and every creepy-crawly ever.

Previously, I'd only been down here for half a second to reaffirm my distaste for dark, damp hovels when Win mentioned he was having a wine cellar put in here and he needed me to see the space.

I'd poked my head down here and told him he could house aliens in it if he wanted, however he wanted. Now I wished I'd paid closer attention to the landscape of things. I didn't even know if there was a window I could get to if I could manage to break the duct tape imprisoning my wrists.

Unfortunately, I couldn't remember how I got here. Maybe this was Win's idea of some kind of surprise spy training?

"Is this Spy Camp 101? Because not funny to entice me to the door for some pizza and wail me in the back of the head. Hey…hold on. How did you wail me in the back of the head? Have you been lying to me about moving big things? Like more than the usual newbie spirit stunts allows? Can you move things, Win?"

I heaved a sigh and let my eyes slide closed again. It was exhausting just to talk. Dang. I was so sleepy.

"Stevie, keep your eyes open. Do not fall back to sleep!" Win barked the order, making my head pop back upward from its decline to my shoulder.

But I felt absolutely no urgency to do as Win suggested at this point. I'm not sure if it was because my head hurt so much, but I was feeling pretty loopy.

There was rustling from upstairs, the door still open, revealing a shaft of light from the kitchen. When I recalled Win's words about my phone, I noted it was indeed smashed on the concrete floor, and then I heard footsteps.

Okay, scratch that. Urgency came in a tidal wave of awareness, hitting me square in the gut.

"Who's up there, Win? What the fudge is going on?" I whispered, fighting panic. As awareness solidified, I began to see my predicament clearly.

Stevie tied up in a damp basement equals bad ju-ju, was my summation in a nutshell.

"Oh, jolly good! You're awake!" A far-too-cheerful voice sang as heavy feet descended on the creaky steps. A man. For sure, it was a man with big feet.

Then I snorted to myself. I was the lamest sleuth ever. Okay, so he was a man and he had big feet. That could be a good quarter of the population.

I squinted when he made an appearance, the light blaring down in front of his form making it hard for me to totally see who was holding me hostage.

"Who are you?"

"The man who's going to kill you, of course," he answered, his accent very clearly British.

In that moment, that stark moment of clarity, everything came together in a big blob of understanding. I knew exactly who he was, because Win's last words before I was tied up came back to me in a flash.

Fish-and-chips man.

But Sally hadn't mentioned he was British… Wouldn't he stick out like a sore thumb in Ebenezer Falls with an accent like that?

He bent down on his haunches beneath the harsh glow of the glaring light bulb in the ceiling, allowing me my first glimpse at my captor.

I hate to admit it. I should be all kinds of freaked out, but he was, as Sally had described, pretty good-looking. Dark hair, thick and falling to just above his chin, blue-blue eyes the color of Caribbean water, with thick eyelashes that made his eyes look like he'd rimmed them in black liner.

And he did smell good. Really good.

I gulped because he also held the pizza delivery kid's hat in his hand, which instantly made me worry he'd killed him, too.

Leaning forward, I asked, "Who are you? I mean, not the part about the guy who's going to kill me. I get that. Your name. What's your name?"

He lifted his square jaw and gave me the once over. "Why does it matter? You're going to die tonight. Names aren't important."

"Well, gravy's sake. Why do you *suppose* it matters? If I'm going to die, I'd at least like to know the name of my killer. It's like a killer courtesy or something."

He barked a laugh, a laugh that suspiciously sounded like Win's…

Well, huh.

"It's Salvatore. Salvatore Finch. Does that ease the stress of dying at the hands of a stranger, Stevie Cartwright?"

A.k.a Sal? The Sal of too much chrome and steel? Naw. How…? Oh boy. It was all coming together for me now.

Win cleared that right up for me. "It's my cousin *Sal*, Stevie! I can't believe I'd forgotten how much he loves fish and chips. It never occurred to me he'd come all the way here from Lancashire. I never made the connection. Especially since he had no idea he was named in the will to begin with."

"Some kind of spy you are," I muttered to Win.

Sal lifted his chin, his eyes narrowing. "Say again?"

The mention of spies made Sal take notice, and if I hoped to consider getting out of here alive, I decided to at least try to disorient him with some ghost talk.

So I sat up straight and enunciated my words. "I was talking to your cousin. I told him he was a crappy spy. He didn't properly decipher a clue. A big one." *A really big one.*

Sal rose in a swift movement, his eyes scanning the entire length of the basement. "He can't be here. My only cousin is dead, you sod!"

I smiled as though I had a secret I wasn't willing to share, fighting to keep myself calm. "But he is. In fact, he just told me you come from Lancashire. Is it nice there? I've always wanted to go to England, you know. I'm a little put out I'll miss it because you're going to kill me. Do you think you can see England from up there?"

Sal's blue eyes went icy-hot when he raised his hand, fist balled, and clocked me in the eye, knocking me and the chair I sat in backward.

With no way to brace myself, I fell to the concrete floor, cracking my head against the hard surface.

But the good news was, the rope around my feet had loosened. I mean, good in that, maybe I could give him a swift kick in his taters before he annihilated me.

If I was going out, I at least wanted to do it kicking and screaming—literally—so I worked at untangling my feet. My head swam and I think my eyeballs crossed as the sharp sting of my head bouncing off the concrete floor swirled around my skull.

But that didn't stop Win from chewing my ear off. "Stevie, listen to me!" Win barked his order, as usual.

"Win! Shh!" I said on a wince. "I'm trying to get to know your cousin, is it, Sal? Right, you're Win's cousin?"

"Stevie…" he warned.

Sal was suddenly eerily calm. He yanked my chair back up, bringing me with it, driving me back into the hard seat with rough hands without even noticing I'd managed to almost free myself from the rope. "You know what I think the bigger question is here, Stevie? How do you know who I am?"

Rolling my eyes even as my head swam in dizzy circles and my face throbbed, I stated the obvious. "Duh. I just told you—your cousin. Though, one quick question. How did you get past Sally at the B&B with that accent? She never mentioned it."

Sal's grin was sly, a total pat on his own back. "Lots and lots of American television as a child. Smart, right?" he asked in what was definitely a very good American accent.

"Was it you I saw going into Madam Z's store in the Burberry trench coat?"

"Stevie! This isn't show and tell time," Win griped, his tone urgent.

Sal grinned, his gorgeous eyes shiny and bright. "You can never go wrong with a Burberry. Was it *you* poking around in her store the other day?"

"Well, seeing as we're sharing confessions. Yeah. I managed to squeeze out of that tiny window in her bathroom. Imagine that, huh?"

Sal cocked an eyebrow. "Imagine that."

"You planted Madam Z's Senior Alert necklace here then tipped the cops off anonymously with that awesomely done American accent, didn't you?"

"I did indeed." And then he wiped the smile from his face. "Now, I repeat, how do you know who I am?"

"Because of Win."

"*Who's Win?*"

"Oh, wait. Maybe you don't call him Win? I mean *Crispin*. Your cousin the spy? You know him, right? Evasive, shady, kinda snippy and sometimes even snobby. Golly, him and his food requirements alone qualify him as a snob. Anyway, he's here right now. He told me all about how he'd left this house and all his money to you. He was very upset by what he thought you'd do to this house, Sal. He wants to restore it, but he said you'd turn it into a monster of steel and chrome."

"I did say that, didn't I?" Win chuckled, the deep sound settling in my left ear.

I looked to my left and nodded, fighting another wince of pain. "Yep. You sure did, Win. So he had Madam Zoltar change his will. He did it from the afterlife, too. Crazy, right?"

Sal leaned forward, gripping the top of either side of the chair and leering at me. "Are you mad?"

I paused in thought. "Define 'mad'. Do you mean as in appointments-with-psychiatrists-and-meds mad? Or like angry mad? You British have different meanings for stuff than we do. For instance, we call—"

"*Who* are you talking to? Crispin's dead!" he screamed at me, the veins in his forehead popping out.

I hitched my jaw at his face, fighting fear with a glib approach. "You have a little something in the corner of your mouth."

He gave the chair a hard shake to let me know he meant business. Man, he was strong. It was as if I only weighed fifty pounds soaking wet—which is awesome if he's your boyfriend, because believe me, I weigh at least a hundred pounds more. But not so awesome if he's your killer.

"How do you know him? I've never heard of you before."

"That's because I'd never heard of Win before he popped into my life just after you killed Madam Zoltar."

"Is *Win* his super-secret spy name—a code name for Mr. Bigshot?" Sal sneered, his handsome face twisting into a mask of hatred.

"It's what he told me to call him—"

"*You lie!*" he bellowed, those thick veins of his popping back out again—all along the column of his neck and his forehead.

Win whistled in my ear. "Stevie! Stop taunting him right now. He's not right in the head. I'm ordering you to stop this instant! You're only provoking him."

But the heck I was going to die before I had some answers. "Swear it on a blueberry Pop-Tart, Sal. Those are my favorite, BTW. I'm a medium. Sort of like Madam Zoltar was. You know, the nice old lady you killed? What I can't figure out is *why* you killed her. What did she have that you wanted?"

Why wasn't I able to put this all together? I was struggling to figure out what Madam Z had to do with Sal, and how he'd come to kill a woman he didn't even know.

Reaching behind him, Sal yanked something from his waistband. Something I knew couldn't be good. When he held up his hand, I saw the gun, viciously gleaming silver.

Perfect.

Sal waved it at me before jamming it in my face. "Does any of it matter? You're going to die, Stevie Cartwright. Just like Madam Zoltar."

Chapter 16

"Waitwaitwaaait!" I screamed in panic as he took a step backward. "I thought we had a killing-courtesy thing here? All I want to know is why you killed Madam Z! Also, maybe if you told me why you want me dead, I'd rest much more peacefully. So c'mon. It's like a last-wish thing. Please? *Pretty please?*" I fought the tremble in my voice with every word I spoke.

Sal made a pouty face at me. Now he had a secret and it appeared as though he was rather enjoying this turn of events. "Haven't you figured it out yet? She did something. Something *very* bad. She changed Crispin's will and put your name in it."

Ice coursed through my veins, icy talons of fear. "*How* do you know that?" Both Win and I asked simultaneously.

Sal looked like he'd decided to play my game when he smiled and said, "A woman called me. Quite out of the blue, in fact. According to her, the change had already been made. Imagine my surprise when I realized he'd originally left everything to me, and I had to make it here to quaint little Ebenezer Falls before the will was opened and read if I hoped to change it back. Getting here all the way from across the pond in enough time proved stressful. I was dreadfully late."

My heart crashed against my ribs hard, but I kept pushing for more answers. "What woman?"

Sal waved the gun in the air in a dismissive gesture. "Bah. I don't know. She called anonymously. Isn't that always the way? But she certainly knew a lot about yooou," he drawled, then threw his dark head back and laughed at himself. "She told me, under Cris's instruction, this Madam Zoltar had changed the sole beneficiary from my name to yours. I didn't know anything about his will or a house, but still, I couldn't figure out why Cris would do such a thing. I was so hurt. Devastated, in fact. Why leave all of his possessions to a complete stranger? We're family! So who are you to him, Stevie Cartwright?"

I ignored his question and shook my head, tears stinging the corners of my eyes. "But you killed her a day *after* Win's will was read. Why would you do that when there was nothing you or she could have done to change it anyway?" This was all so senseless. Madam Z never had to die at all.

He used the butt of the gun to scratch his forehead. "Oh, she carried on about that. She told me the will had already been changed and there was nothing I could do. That made me mad. *So mad.* The caller did say someone despicable was going to get their hands on his money if I didn't change the will back. To think, if my flight hadn't been delayed, I'd have arrived on time and I could have changed it back and no one would have had to die."

Who? Who had called Sal to warn him? Who could have possibly known? Win was already dead by the time he'd asked MZ to change his will. Would one of my coven do something so awful? Had someone else been communicating with the afterlife in my stead?

And then it hit me in a sick wave of understanding, but Sal was still droning on and I had to focus.

"Mr. Bigshot, always wandering around like he was James Bond reincarnated while I worked a menial nine-to-five, slogging back and forth on the tube day in, day out. Everything was some important secret with Cris. My nana used to gush all the time about him to her friends and I was sick of it! Even when we were young blokes, he always thought he was better than all of us—me especially!"

Win sighed in my ear, grating and long. "Still slagging me off even in death. Sal is a jealous Nancy. Always whining about something. Surely you can see why I didn't want to foist him upon the good people of Ebenezer Falls?"

I shook my head as though it would extract Win. "I still don't understand why you killed her, Sal? She was a harmless old lady who'd never hurt anyone." The thought tore at my heart.

Liza's face flashed in front of my eyes, her sorrow, her raw pain. And that made me angry. *So angry*.

Sal became agitated again. In fact, every time I mentioned him killing Madam Z, he became edgier. Now he paced back and forth in front of me. "Because she wouldn't tell me whom he'd given all this to! That's why!" He spread his arms wide to encompass the basement. "*You* got all his money and this shambles of a house and I got nothing! I was going to force her to change the will back until I found out the deed was already done and there was nothing I could do about it. That made me *furious*, Stevie. So furious. If not for you, she'd still be alive. It's all *your* fault. You have no one to blame but yourself!"

I swallowed hard. "So you made her call the Senior Alert line to keep help from coming and then strangled her to death?"

Sal instantly stopped pacing, his focus solely on me, his blue eyes soft and melty. "I promised not to kill her, you know—if she called off the cops." He smiled as though the memory were a fond one, making my stomach somersault.

"I'll kill him," Win growled, harsh and angry. "*Kill him*."

But I remained silent, my mouth dry. I wasn't sure I could keep Sal talking long enough before I vomited at his filthy feet.

"But I gotta give it to the old bird; she wouldn't tell me whose name was on that will, no matter what I did. Doesn't matter. I found a copy of it just this afternoon. Took me a couple of days, but it was easy enough once the cops cleared out. Lost a nice pen in the process, too. The pen *Win* had his secretary send me for Christmas one year, the braggart."

The Montblanc. How could Win not have made the connection?

"Before you go accusing me of not catching that clue, I have no idea what my secretary sends to anyone for Christmas," Win defended. "And who knew this sod could mimic an American accent?"

Running his hands through his hair, Sal shook his head, as though he regretted killing Madam Z. "I couldn't let her live, of course. She'd have ratted me out to the authorities. Boy, but she was tough. Held out right until the very end. Right up until the bitter end, in fact. Struggled so hard, she jammed her foot against that pedal she had under the table—blew the socket right out of the wall!"

Oh God. He truly was insane.

But what left me feeling the absolute worst? Madam Z had been protecting *me* even before she knew who I was. Because of Win.

As my stomach turned, I knew I had to figure a way out of this basement. I didn't know how I was going to do that, but Sal couldn't be allowed to walk free.

Licking my lips, I swallowed hard and forced myself to ask, "So…how is killing me going to help you, Sal? You won't be able to get your hands on Crispin's money. It'll go into probate forever. The legal red tape will be a nightmare."

He shook a finger at me, his eyes almost wild, his brow covered in a think sheen of sweat. "Ah, but that's where you're wrong. You're going to sign everything over to me in your brand new will, Stevie. Lock, stock and millions of Mr. Showoff's money!"

I shook my head. The hell I would. "I won't do it. You can't make me."

He reached down and pulled up the leg of his jeans, dragging a knife from his sock to hold it up against the light. "You will if I cut your fingers off one by one. You'll give in exactly the way Madam Zoltar did, crying and begging for your life."

"Stevie, we have to do something rash and we have to do it now." Win's voice was calm, but I was sure he could see as well as I could, Sal was falling further down the rabbit hole.

"Stevie? You here? Brought you some coffee to cheer you up!"

Forrest?

I froze, that icy course of blood streaming through my veins again as Sal's head popped up and his eyes went wide.

"Stevie, you must act! Listen closely. The moment Sal turns his back to find out who's calling you, grab that chair and hit him. Hit him *hard*, Stevie, and make it count. Use everything you've got!"

I nodded and gulped. *Hit him with the chair, hit him with the chair.*

"Stevie? Where are you?"

Sal's eyes narrowed, his mouth turning to a thin line, and then he did just as Win suspected. "Don't make a sound, or whoever that is will die, just like you," he threatened.

He turned to head for the steps—and with a whoosh of air and a silent prayer to the goddesses, I slid from the chair, grabbed it with my imprisoned hands, lifted it high and nailed him on the side of his deranged head.

"Run, Stevie!" Win hollered. "Run and don't look back!"

I did as I was told, fighting the wave after wave of dizziness as I attempted to climb the steps. "Forrest! Get help!" I screamed upward, my voice raspy and tight.

Just as I reached the top of the stairs, I saw Forrest, his face slathered in his surprise. "Stevie! Are you okay?"

The moment the words flew from his mouth was the moment Win yelled in my ear, "Tell Forrest to duck!"

"Forrest, duck!"

I did as Win told me just before a shot rang out that, to my horror, took Forrest to the ground with a thud that shook the rafters of the house.

But I didn't have time to react before Sal was grabbing at my ankles, trying to drag me back down the stairs.

"Roll over, Stevie! Roll over and kick his hand with the gun then uppercut with the heel of your foot to his jaw!" Win directed.

Again, I did as I was told, acting merely on adrenaline and British spy advice. Rolling to my back, I whacked at Sal's hand as he dragged me down, my head banging against each tread as we went.

I whooped a yelp of triumph when I successfully knocked the gun from his hand and followed up with the hardest kick I could manage just beneath his jaw.

Sal howled when my heel made contact and he fell back down a few steps, giving me enough time to roll back over and scurry the rest of the way up the stairs.

I tripped over Forrest's big body, his arm bleeding from the gunshot, his forehead following suit with a big gash in it.

"Don't stop now, Stevie—he won't trouble himself with Forrest. It's *you* he wants. You have to run! Sal's right behind you!"

"*Where?*" I screeched into the kitchen, trying to break free from the duct tape on my wrists, but I couldn't remember a dang thing Win told me about how to do it.

"Enzo's hammer, by the microwave. Grab it now and hide! I'll get Bel to use Forrest's phone to call 9-1-1. Do it now!"

I managed to grab the hammer just in the nick of time, almost fumbling it before grasping it securely and running through the kitchen into the dining room.

I thanked every God available to my memory Win had decided to knock down the wall between the kitchen and the dining room as I scooted around the corner, my feet plowing over discarded nails.

As my heart pounded in my chest like the hammer I was holding, my eyes wildly searched for somewhere to run. The wind outside howled, crying out, the frigid air coming from the door Forrest must have left open.

"Stevie!" Sal hollered, his voice echoing through the emptiness of the house. "You can't get away from me!"

"You can, Stevie. You will!" Win urged. "He's hurt. You cuffed him on his head but good. He's dizzy and stumbling. Use that to your advantage."

"Stevie!" Sal wailed my name again, his voice closer. "You're going to die tonight!"

"Where?" I whispered, looking toward the set of windows in the dining room.

"No! Not the windows. There's nowhere for you to run in all that mud. No neighbor nearby to help. Bel's dialing 9-1-1 now, but you have no choice but to go up, Stevie. Hurry! Get up the stairs and we'll catch him by surprise!"

Sal had gone silent now, so silent, if not for the howling wind, he'd hear me gasping for breath.

Up. Go up. I snuck around the corner of the dining room, poking my head around it to see the stairs, trying to keep my ragged, fear-filled breathing to a minimum. My eye ached like the dickens, making everything feel off kilter.

When I saw the coast was clear, I ran like the hounds of hell were nipping at my heels, clamping my mouth shut when I hit a jagged patch of wood on the stairs.

I'd just made it to the top where the landing met the steps when Sal's heavy feet touched the first tread. His roar of anger tearing through the air had me biting the inside of my cheek to keep from screaming in terror.

I almost couldn't make my feet move, but Win was there again. "Hide, Stevie! Choose a room, get into it and around the corner of the doorframe. If he gets to you before the police arrive, whack him again. Run, Stevie!"

I flew down the long, dark hallway to the left, scooting into the second room and directly around the corner just as sirens pealed, piercing the night air. My eye throbbed, my vision becoming worse by the second.

Sal's footsteps grew closer, pounding, driving, running right past the room I was hidden in, and I almost breathed a sigh of relief, thinking Sal had gone another way, until Win bellowed, "Stevie, now!"

I whacked at the air, not even sure what I was whacking at, it was so dark, but I got him good on some fleshy part of his body I couldn't distinguish. Judging from Sal's howl of discontent, it hurt. As my eyes began to adjust, I pushed my way past him, using all my strength to get out the door.

I managed to fumble to the hallway, crashing against the wall before I took off running again, unsure where to go next.

"Stevie! I'm going to tell you to do something crazy, but it'll buy you time until the police get here! You can't let him get his hands on you or he'll strangle you before the police arrive. See that rope on the scaffolding at the edge of the broken railing to the stairs? Grab it, push off the step then make like Tarzan and swing!"

"Are you insane? I'll never make that! Have I mentioned I failed gym?" I cried as the rope he was talking about came into view. It was hanging from the highest point of the entryway scaffolding that went all the way across to the wall along the stairs—the entryway I'd thought would eventually be so beautiful, not where I'd leap to my death.

Uh, no way.

But Sal's feet were coming faster now, his insidious footsteps, the rasp of his breath lending to sheer terror like I've never known.

So I did it. I ran for that rope like it was the only thing to grab on to that would keep me from falling off the edge of the planet.

The coarse material ripped at my hands as I gripped it, wrapping it around my restrained wrists, panic making me push off the step just as Sal grabbed at my right foot, his fingers slipping off my ankle with a howl of rage.

"Ahhh!" As I flew across the entryway and headed into the parlor, where I was sure I was going to fall to my death, I screamed again.

My scream was matched by Sal's bone-chilling howl, making me swivel my head to see him fall head first over the banister. His skull hit the table saw with a sick thud before he landed on the entryway floor, a pool of blood spreading out behind his ebony hair.

But Win gave me yet another order. "Don't look back again, Stevie! Look down and the minute you see the parlor floor, drop, tuck, roll!"

Honest, as I flew over the entryway and into the parlor, I'm not sure I had a choice *but* to drop because my entire being shook with fear.

"Drop, Stevie! Drop now!"

So, I dropped, probably fifteen feet or so, definitely much higher than the window at Madam Z's, and fell to the floor on my arm in a crumpling heap.

So much for tuck and roll.

Then there were flashlights and sirens and people yelling and Sandwich on crutches, kneeling down beside me. "Stevie! Don't move. Stay right there," he ordered, suddenly sounding incredibly authoritative. "Here, let me get the tape off your wrists."

But I had to see if Sal was really dead, so I sat up, my body bruised and battered, my feet bloody and raw.

Win's warmth surrounded me all at once. "Stevie. Don't look anymore. You've seen enough. *Please*."

"But Sal…what if—"

"He didn't," Win reassured me in soft words. "He's gone. There's nothing to fear."

Sandwich confirmed what Win told me as he took the tape from my wrists with gentle hands. "It's all okay now, Stevie. There's nothing to worry about where he's concerned."

And then I remembered Forrest, his arm wounded from a bullet, his head gushing blood. "Forrest!"

The paramedics arrived with gurneys and blood pressure cuffs, heading toward the kitchen, but I had to see for myself if Forrest was all right.

I fought to move them out of my way, but Sandwich was back in my line of vision again. "It's okay, Stevie. Forrest's gonna be just fine. We got the pizza delivery kid, too. He's okay. Now, let the people do their job and make sure you're okay. You took quite a shiner to the eye. Doc at the hospital's gonna wanna look at that."

Heaving a sigh of relief, I allowed the paramedics to put me on a gurney and wheel me out of the house to the ambulance.

"Do as Sardine says," Win said. "I'll be here the whole way. Promise."

And he was, right up until the moment they wanted to admit me. But I had Belfry to consider and no way to explain his existence. So after giving the police another statement, I took the script for pain meds, promised to see the eye doctor for my trashed eyeball, tucked the sling for my sprained arm against my body and let Sandwich drive me home.

"Wish you'd have at least stayed the night, Stevie. Your eye's all kinda colors," he remarked with a smile just as dawn was breaking over the horizon, the drizzle of a new day arriving in the way of splotches of rain.

"What kind of accused murderer would I be if I couldn't take a right hook to the eye?" I joked, forcing myself to keep things light.

"About that," Sandwich said, his face somber, his eyes tired. "I was just doing my job. Sometimes it's hard to separate that from friendship, Stevie. I have to keep things professional, but I never thought you hurt that nice lady."

I smiled until it hurt my eye. "Are we friends now, Sandwich?"

He held out his hand and grinned. "You bet. Now lemme get you up this mudslide and inside where it's warm."

"And how are you going to do that with a sprained ankle? It's enough you already did it once today. I'll be fine, Sandwich. Promise. You go home and get some rest." I propped open the door and dropped out of the police cruiser.

Sandwich held up a hand and waved to me just before I turned to fight my way up those crumbling stairs. "Driveway, Crispin Alistair Winterbottom. Before we put coffee-urinating sculptures of David and waterfalls in the kitchen—a driveway, *please*."

He cackled his rich laugh. "A driveway for the lady it is."

I successfully made it to the front steps to find Enzo waiting for me, steaming cup of coffee in hand, the first smile I'd seen on his face since I met him.

"Thought you could use this," he said, gruff and short. "Heard all the commotion on the scanner and came right over. Took care of that mess, too. Police said I could after they finished up here. Didn't want you coming home to that."

Tears welled in my eyes, tears of gratitude. "Oh, Enzo, thank you so much. I..." I couldn't finish my sentence as he led me inside where, as promised, everything was cleaned up.

"Nah, you don't have to thank me. You go get some rest. I won't be bangin' around down here much today, but I'll be here if ya need me." With that, he sauntered down the hall to the kitchen, leaving me with more thank yous on my lips.

"Let's get you your medication, a hot bath and then bed," Win suggested.

I nodded, taking my coffee up the steps, avoiding the rope, and heading straight to my bedroom.

Upon entry, I was thrilled to find a small table by the bed with aspirin and a squeaky-clean glass for water. "Man, Enzo really thought of everything, huh?"

"He's a prince among thieves," Win remarked.

Belfry flew at me, landing on my shoulder and snuggling against my neck with a sigh. "That was some close call, Stevie! You scared the pants off me."

I rubbed my cheek against his soft body as I made my way into the bathroom. "You don't wear pants."

"Doesn't mean you can't scare me. You okay?"

Setting my coffee on the edge of the cracked sink, I nodded. "I'm alive, thanks to Win and you. If you hadn't called 9-1-1, Bel..." I shuddered at the thought before forcing myself to shake it off.

"Say that again?"

"I said—"

"Not you, Stevie. Hold on one second. I'm getting something..."

Leaning back against the sink, I took a sip of the most delicious coffee ever and waited.

Suddenly, Win's warmth surrounded me again, only this time it came with a very different feeling. There were all sorts of emotions mingling with the gentle nudge I'd come to realize was Win's way of comforting me.

I stood up straight, the hair at the nape of my neck standing on end. "Win? What's going on?"

He cleared his throat. "It's Madam Zoltar, Stevie." His voice was thick, chock full of the usual richness, but richer, if that were possible.

"Did you tell her we did it, Win?" I asked, my own voice hitching.

"I did. She says thank you. Thank you for everything. Oh, she's brilliantly clear now, Stevie. She sounds smashing."

I smiled as a lone tear slipped from my eye. "Tell her I'll check in on Liza from time to time, would you?"

"She asked if you'd do her a small favor," he said, his words almost sounding choked.

"Anything," I murmured.

"She has a message for Chester."

That warmth I had come to find familiar heightened, as though someone had thrown a log on the fire, making it leap with a sudden burst of heat. This warmth encompassed not just my physical being, but settled deep within my soul, and words—words of gratitude and direction—popped into my brain as though MZ had dropped them in a mail slot.

And everything was clear—so clear.

"Tell her of course I will." I couldn't say anything more, words escaped me, and as I stroked Bel's tiny head, I felt the link I'd once felt to the afterlife again. It was weak and thready, but it was still there briefly, before it evaporated and slipped away.

"She's gone over," Win whispered low.

I smiled and nodded as more tears fell down my face. "I know…"

And then both Win and I sighed a happy sigh—*together*.

Two Weeks Later

I sat with Win on our newly installed front porch steps, enjoying the warmth of the sun on an unusually, unseasonably bright day in March, grateful my vision was still intact after the right hook I'd taken from Sal.

I'd been exonerated of all charges, especially since Forrest had heard Sal tell me he killed Madam Z. His statement to that effect was the final nail in Sal's coffin and officially closed the case. Forrest was healing nicely, though he'd groused about the four stitches in his head while we shared a cup of that long-awaited coffee just yesterday.

I'd just come back from the doctor, who'd assured me my vision was still 20/20 and the fracture behind my eye was healing nicely. The sprain in my arm was almost one hundred percent, too.

I grabbed the bag from Target and pulled out a frame with a debonair man's picture used for the insert. He had steely-blue eyes, hair the color of a starless Texas night and a chiseled jaw.

"New boyfriend?" Win asked.

"Nope. He's you."

"I beg your pardon?"

"He's you. I'm tired of talking to the air, Win, and seeing as you won't tell me anything about you and what you look like, I'll just use this. Every time I talk to you, I'll break out this picture frame, and this way I'll have a face to go with all that snippy British sophistication."

He laughed in my ear. "I'm not snippy."

I held up the black frame with crisp edges, turning it around against the sun. "He's cute, don't you think? Very spy-like."

Win scoffed. "I look nothing like that. Nothing."

I clucked my tongue. "That's too bad. He's pretty cute. So show me a picture of what you really look like and let *me* decide if you look like him."

"I told you, all in due time, Stevie."

Yeah. He'd said that about how he was able to communicate with me, too. *All in due time, Stevie. When the time is right, Stevie.*

Truthfully, I didn't really mind him not sharing his past. Sure, I was endlessly curious about how he'd died and what he looked like, but I could wait because I liked him. He made me laugh. We'd spent a lot of time together while I recuperated, and between him and Belfry, they'd helped me begin to shape this new life of mine.

I didn't want to rock that boat just yet, so I'd let it rest. I hadn't scoured the Internet for information about him or the prior owner of the house out of respect.

For the immediate future, I was learning things about myself I never knew. I'd begun to take a yoga class or two when realizing how out of shape I was after my encounter with Sal, taking it slow because of my sprained arm.

I took long walks by the shores of the Sound. I sat and watched the waves from my bedroom window almost every day now. I spent my nights watching Netflix or scouring the Internet for items Win wanted for the house while Belfry gave us his opinion about them whether we wanted it or not.

When everyone in town found out what happened with Sal, as easily as they'd scorned me for allegedly killing one of their own, the flip side of it was, they'd welcomed me back into the fold with open arms. Casseroles and apologies were what Ebenezer Falls was all about, and I had plenty of the former in my shiny French-door chef's refrigerator delivered just yesterday.

I'd been invited to several functions, bake sales, house parties, and any number of different celebrations once I recuperated, and I intended to start throwing myself back into the world again very soon.

For now, I was content to just breathe easier knowing Belfry and I had a place to hang our hats and I wasn't going to die if I wasn't a witch.

That didn't mean I wasn't going to hope someday, somehow, I'd find a way to rejoin my coven, but if this was my life for the moment, I'd take it.

Looking out over the wide expanse of what would eventually be the front lawn, but was now mostly mud, I smiled as Chester Sherwood waved to me from a horseshoe section he'd cordoned off with tomato plant sticks and string. He made his way to the front porch when he saw me, his stout body taking each step with forceful determination.

"He looks quite well, doesn't he?" Win commented.

I nodded, pulling my knees to my chest and smiling fondly as Chester hiked up his signature red suspenders. "He looks great. I heard a rumor he was seeing Lavinia Stapleton, but she can't seem to get him to commit to being her full-time boyfriend."

"Maybe our message will help him let go?"

Smiling fondly, I bobbed my head. "I hope so."

"Mornin', Stevie!" Chester chirped, his eyes bright with the prospect of helping me design the front garden. "Ya look good, kiddo. Told ya that doc would fix ya right up."

I grinned at him, tucking my hair behind my ears. "He did indeed. But forget me, how are *you*, Casanova? I hear you've been courting one Lavinia Stapleton."

He blushed and tweaked my cheek with his calloused fingers. "She's a fine old gal. Makes a helluva chicken casserole, too."

I'd given my next words a lot of thought, about how I'd approach the subject of Violet, Chester's deceased wife. I'd decided after his relationship with Madam Zoltar and his wish to believe in the afterlife because of his wife, he'd be okay with what I had to pass on.

"You know, Chester, I had a dream the other night. You know who was in it?"

"Better not be me. I'm too old for a pretty spry thing like you."

Chuckling, I said, "If only I was forty years older, but you weren't in the dream. Though, I think it had to do with you. Now, Madam Zoltar? She was in my dream. Clear as day, happy, smiling, wearing a really pretty caftan in teal blue with splashes of pink. Wanna know what she said to me in the dream? Because it was the funniest thing, and I'm not sure I understand it…"

Chester's eyes showed interest when he nodded. "I sure like hearin' she's lookin' well. What'd she say?"

I grabbed his hand and held it. "She said she wanted me to tell you that Violet is as lovely as you said she was, and maybe even prettier than you described. And then she said something I don't understand. She said Violet told her to tell you, if she got to the lilac bush down by her father's farm before you did, she'd wait for you."

Chester took his white hat with the brown band around it off his head and held it at his heart, his eyes faraway. "*She really said that?*" he asked, his voice hoarse.

Squeezing his hand, I nodded and smiled, swallowing hard so I wouldn't burst into tears. "She did," I whispered.

Chester visibly gulped, using his shoulder to wipe at his eyes. "Used to meet her down there when we were courtin'. It was our favorite spot, and it's where I proposed. It was our little secret place...nobody knows about it but us two..." His voice hitched, thick with emotion.

And that was how I knew I'd done the right thing.

Hopping up, I hugged him hard and he hugged me back. Then he set me from him, his hands at my waist, and said, "You're a good girl, Stevie. Don't let anyone tell ya otherwise."

"Told you I'd make you like me eventually," I teased, dropping a kiss on his cheek before he wandered back down to the garden, a watery smile of wonder on his face.

Brushing the tears from my eyes with my thumb, I plopped back down on the steps and sighed.

"You're a kind woman, Stevie Cartwright."

"I bet you say that to all the people you've dumped in the middle of a murder."

"Funny you should mention murder, because I have a question about that night with Sal. Do you think you're up to it?"

I didn't shrink from the subject of Sal at all; I wanted to face it head-on so I could rid myself of the terror he'd instilled in me. I wouldn't let him haunt me. "I'm up for it."

"Who do you suppose called him to tip him off about the change in my will? My suspicions lead me to wonder if it was someone from Paris?"

That was the one thing I still hadn't come to terms with, but I had my suspicions, too. "I have a horrible feeling it was Adam Westfield's wife, Ann. He might not be here on this plane, but he's a powerful warlock, Win, with plenty of ways to reach out. Because he's instilled such terror in her, if anyone could talk that woman into doing something like that, it's him."

"So powerful he could get a message to her to do something that awful?"

"Well, you're talking to me right now, aren't you? And I'm not even a witch anymore. If what you say is true, and this experiment you were so vague about is what helped you contact a mere mortal, it's obviously possible. If Adam had even an inkling Sal would come after me, if he sensed evil in Sal and a way to utilize it, he'd do it just because he wants the rest of my days to suck butt. But that also means you need to watch *your* back, Win. If Adam was responsible for Sal, if he can reach out in death, he can certainly get to you in the afterlife."

"I don't like hearing this, Stevie. That he can manipulate people from beyond the grave in such a dire manner is reason for concern. As for me? I'd love to see him try."

"We have no way to know for sure. Just keep your eyes and ears open and we'll revisit if necessary. Okay?" If I lingered too long on the kind of reach Adam Westfield did or didn't have, I'd never get out of bed again.

"Done."

"Okay, let's talk happier stuff. Like my visit to the doctor."

Win's laughter, warm and husky, echoed in my ear. "So what say the doctor? Are we fit as a fiddle again?"

Closing my eyes, I inhaled the scent of the Sound as the sun beat down on my head. "Well, we're fit. The fiddle is questionable. My vision's fine and the sprain in my arm from that crazy bungee jump I did from the rope on the scaffolding is all good, too. I'm healing well."

"And how is your mental state, Stevie? How are you handling someone trying to kill you?"

I'll admit, I'd had some rough nights since that one when Sal almost killed me, but if I woke in a cold sweat, Belfry was always there to soothe me. And all I had to do was call on Win, and he dropped the philandering he was always bragging he was doing on Plane Pick-Up, and talked me down.

All in all, I was mending in more ways than one ,and Win and I were forming a friendship I'd come to rely on…dare I say even enjoy? Unless he's sticking his nose in swatches of paint and light fixtures. Then I wish for the old days when I could zap a pestering spirit off to another plane.

"I feel pretty good. You've been a big part of my healing. Thank you for that, Win."

His warm aura surrounded me when he said, "Excellent. Then we begin spy-training camp tomorrow."

I frowned. "Do I have to eat wheatgrass and raw eggs for breakfast to attend spy-training camp?"

"No. Nothing so extreme. Just some raw liver and pig's feet smoothies. They make for a strong spy."

I laughed at him, my giggle floating on the ocean breeze. "So how are *you* these days, International Man of Intrigue? I feel like everything's been way too much about *me* lately, and I've forgotten to ask how you're doing."

"I'm right as rain."

"So, listen, after I went to the doctor's today, I did a little something."

"Please tell me it wasn't a trip to the new vintage clothing store you couldn't quit nattering on about. You can afford to buy all those designer labels you so covet, Stevie—brand new, in fact."

"Ah. But it's not as much fun if there's no hunt for your prey. No big rush at your coup. If I just buy whatever I wanted, there'd be no thrill."

"I imagine someday I'll find this trait of yours endearing. For now, tell me what you did? More shoes from Betsy Whoever for three bucks?"

I pulled a paper from my pocket and unfolded it, holding it up. "This is what I did after the doctor's today."

Win's pause left me certain he was as stunned as I'd hoped he would be. I just hoped it was a happy stunned.

"*You bought Madam Zoltar's?*"

"Yep, lock, stock and crystal ball. I thought maybe, if you were game, I could be Madam Zoltar 2.0 or some variation, and we could help spirits the way I used to, with you as my conduit to the afterlife. This way, I'd be as legit as anyone can be without actually doing the communicating, and we'd both have a purpose—a reason to get up every day. I checked with Liza, to be sure it wouldn't upset her, and she said she'd be thrilled to see the sign lit up again. I mean, that's unless you've decided you want to cross over."

I let him digest for a moment, roll it around in his brain. He was, after all, the one I'd have to rely on to help me make contact.

Holding up the picture frame, I asked, "So, Crispin Alistair Winterbottom—you in?"

"I think I am, Stevie Like-Nicks-the-Singer. I think I am. But there's one small thing I'd like to discuss."

"You want rules? We've got scads of 'em. What's one more?"

"No more rules. This is personal."

I crossed my legs in front of me and stretched. "Okay, tell me."

"There's another reason I contacted you, Stevie. It wasn't just about the house and money…"

Maybe this would fill in the blanks for me. Help me to understand what piece of Win's puzzle I was missing. "Then shoot."

"You asked why I hadn't crossed over once, and here's really why—I believe I can get back to your plane."

No. No. That wasn't possible. How could he even think that? How did I tell him it was impossible? "How do you plan to accomplish coming back from the dead, Win?"

"I know you think it's improbable, maybe even impossible, but if you were once a real-live witch—spells and cauldrons and all—why couldn't I be reincarnated? Who's to say I can't come back?"

He had a point, but still, I couldn't encourage him. Even though I found I'd like very much for Win to actually be here, I just didn't see how it was possible.

In all the spells I knew, in all the crazy hoodoo I could once conjure as a witch, I'd never witnessed an actual reincarnation. I also still had no answer for how Win was communicating with me if I no longer had my powers.

Yet, here we were…communicating as though he were on this plane.

"I can see your skepticism, and for now we can leave this in a box somewhere—all tied up. But regardless, I know in my gut there's a way. *I know.* And when the time comes, I'd like your help."

My chest went all tight and itchy at his conviction, but Win was right. For now it was better we left this topic in a box.

"Fair enough. We'll leave it alone for the time being and focus on helping the other side, with me as MZ Jr."

Belfry yawned when I scooped him from my purse and placed him on my shoulder. "Can I help, too?"

"Would we be the dynamic three-o any other way? We're like *Charlie's Angels* now," I joked.

"I call Sabrina," Win said. "She was the smart one."

"I'll take Farrah. I think I have the hair for it," Belfry added, melting into peals of laughter.

"Well, if this very moment isn't fortuitous. It must be fate," Win commented, a thread of excitement in his voice.

I wrinkled my nose and cocked my head. "What's fortuitous?"

"Shhh, Stevie! I can't hear." Win stopped talking for a moment and then he said, "Whoa, whoa, whoa. Slow down, *mi amigo*. I don't speak Spanish. Turkish, Russian, Latvian, French, and Italian, yes. But my Spanish is rusty. What's that you say about Stevie?" He paused again. "Well, hell. I'll tell her. Of course I'll tell her. Just give me a minute."

I sat up straight now, totally alert. "*Tell me what?*"

"I think we have our first customer, MZ 2.0 and you're never going to believe who it is. You'd better get your turban pressed."

The urgency in Win's voice made my heart kick up a notch. "Well, tell me already. I can't stand the suspense!"

As Win muttered whom he was talking to in my ear, and my eyes went wide with shock, I nodded with purpose. "Tell her we're on it!"

That thrill of hope I'd been experiencing these past couple of weeks returned in a rush of adrenaline. I was coming to terms with my new life as a non-witch, and I was still doing what I'd always loved to do.

Helping people—only now I was doing it with a little help from my friends.

It just didn't get any better than that.

The End

I so hope you enjoyed *Witch Slapped*, and I hope you'll return to Ebenezer Falls and find out whom our intrepid afterlife spy Win is communicating with, how he plans to get back to this plane, how in the fudge he's communicating with Stevie and if our Mini-Spy, Stevie's, always going to remain mortal in Book 2, *Quit Your Witchin'*—the *Witchless in Seattle Mysteries*!

Note from Dakota

I do hope you enjoyed this book, I'd so appreciate it if you'd help others enjoy it too.

Recommend it. Please help other readers find this book by recommending it.

Review it. Please tell other readers why you liked this book by reviewing it at online retailers or your blog. Reader reviews help my books continue to be valued by distributors/resellers. I adore each and every reader who takes the time to write one!

If you love the book or leave a review, please email dakota@dakotacassidy.com so I can thank you with a personal email. Your support means more than you'll ever know! Thank you!

About Dakota

Dakota Cassidy is a *USA Today* bestselling author with over thirty books. She writes laugh-out-loud cozy mysteries, romantic comedy, grab-some-ice erotic romance, hot and sexy alpha males, paranormal shifters, contemporary kick-ass women, and more.

Dakota was invited by Bravo TV to be the Bravoholic for a week, wherein she snarked the hell out of all the Bravo shows. She received a starred review from Publishers Weekly for *Talk Dirty to Me*, won a Romantic Times Reviewers' Choice Award for *Kiss and Hell*, along with many review site recommended reads and reviewer top pick awards.

Dakota lives in the gorgeous state of Oregon with her real life hero and her dogs, and she loves hearing from readers!

Connect with Dakota online:

Twitter: https://twitter.com/DakotaCassidy

Facebook: https://www.facebook.com/DakotaCassidyFanPage

Dakota Cassidy | Witch Slapped

Join Dakota Cassidy's Newsletter, The Tiara Diaries: http://mad.ly/signups/100255/join

eBooks by Dakota Cassidy

Visit Dakota's website at http://www.dakotacassidy.com for more information.

Accidentally Paranormal, a Paranormal Romantic Comedy series

Interview With an Accidental—a free introductory guide to the girls of the Accidentals!

1. The Accidental Werewolf
2. Accidentally Dead
3. The Accidental Human
4. Accidentally Demonic
5. Accidentally Catty
6. Accidentally Dead, Again
7. The Accidental Genie
8. The Accidental Werewolf 2: Something About Harry
9. The Accidental Dragon
10. Accidentally Aphrodite
11. Accidentally Ever After
12. Bearly Accidental
13. How Nina Got Her Fang Back
14. The Accidental Familiar

A Lemon Layne Mystery, a Contemporary Cozy Mystery Series

1. Prawn of the Dead
2. Play That Funky Music White Koi
3. Total Eclipse of the Carp

Witchless In Seattle Mysteries, a Paranormal Cozy Mystery series

1. Witch Slapped
2. Quit Your Witchin'
3. Dewitched
4. The Old Witcheroo

 5. How the Witch Stole Christmas

Wolf Mates, a Paranormal Romantic Comedy series

 1. An American Werewolf In Hoboken

 2. What's New, Pussycat?

 3. Gotta Have Faith

 4. Moves Like Jagger

 5. Bad Case of Loving You

A Paris, Texas Romance, a Paranormal Romantic Comedy series

 1. Witched At Birth

 2. What Not to Were

 3. Witch Is the New Black

 4. White Witchmas

Non-Series

 1. Whose Bride Is She Anyway?

 2. Polanski Brothers: Home of Eternal Rest

 3. Sexy Lips 66

The Hell, a Paranormal Romantic Comedy series

 1. Kiss and Hell

 2. My Way to Hell

The Plum Orchard, a Contemporary Romantic Comedy series

 1. Talk This Way

 2. Talk Dirty to Me

 3. Something to Talk About

 4. Talking After Midnight

The Ex-Trophy Wives, a Contemporary Romantic Comedy series

 1. You Dropped a Blonde On Me

 2. Burning Down the Spouse

 3. Waltz This Way

Printed in Great Britain
by Amazon